DANNY ORLIS

AND

HAL'S GREAT VICTORY

DANNY ORLIS

AND

HAL'S GREAT VICTORY

BERNARD PALMER

Please note that several books in the Danny Orlis series are published by Sword of the Lord Publications and are available for purchase on their website, www.swordbooks.com.

Aneko Press Youth

www.anekopress.com

Aneko Press, Life Sentence Publishing, and our logos are trademarks of Life Sentence Publishing, Inc.
203 E. Birch Street
P.O. Box 652
Abbotsford, WI 54405

JUVENILE FICTION / Religious / Christian / Action & Adventure

Paperback ISBN: 979-8-88936-002-5

eBook ISBN: 979-8-88936-003-2

10 9 8 7 6 5 4 3 2 1

Available where books are sold

CONTENTS

Ch. 1: Danny's Problem...1

Ch. 2: Jim Meets Doug 7

Ch. 3: Game Summed Up, Gordy Blake.....................17

Ch. 4: Danny and Kay Sponsor Young People's.....................23

Ch. 5: A Great Field of Service 31

Ch. 6: Hal Hadn't Planned It at All 39

Ch. 7: There Is a Way to Help 49

Ch. 8: Hal's Problems Multiply..................................59

Ch. 9: Jim Brings an Accusation 67

Ch. 10: Jim Has a Lesson to Learn.........................77

Ch. 11: Late for Dinner 85

Ch. 12: Big Ed Goes Home 95

Ch. 13: "To Pray and Not Faint" 101

CHAPTER 1

DANNY'S PROBLEM

Danny Orlis followed the mine supervisor to the door and closed it behind him. He turned and for a moment or two he stood there staring at his young wife, Kay. Disbelief still stood in his eyes.

"Did you hear what he said, Kay?" he asked. "We'll be living at Gluymon, Ontario. That means we'll be able to get home a lot more often."

Kay reached up and straightened his collar. He captured her hands. "It's wonderful," she replied.

"I can hardly believe it's true," Danny continued. "We're going to be living close enough to the Angle so that I'll be able to hunt and fish there and do all the things I used to do."

Kay's happy face grew pensive. "Of course there's Hal Seybold. What will happen to him after we leave Tanbark?"

The smile left Danny's eyes. "Now that," he said," is something I don't like to think about."

He ran his stubby fingers through his hair. "And what about Jim? Would he be able to live with us if we move?"

"I don't see why not," Kay countered. "The town would have schools, wouldn't it?"

"Eventually. But it's a new town. There might not be schools or teachers yet."

Kay Orlis' disappointment was reflected in her manner. "Oh, Danny," she exclaimed. "I've been counting so much on having Jim stay with us."

Danny grinned. "Now, Kay," he said, "don't get so fussed up. We don't even know what there is in Gluymon; we won't know until we get there."

He crossed to a chair and sat down. "There's one good thing. Jim is already in school. It isn't as though we had to get the matter settled today."

They were interrupted by a timid knock on the door. Hal Seybold came in. He was the boy Danny had just led to Christ in the wilderness area north of the little mining community.

"How are you, Hal?" Danny asked, opening the door wide.

The boy's lips quivered. "I–I had to sneak over. Dad would whale me if he knew I was over here."

Danny's face grew serious. "We like to have you come, Hal," he said. "You're welcome here any time, but you must not do things against your dad's wishes.

You're a Christian. You have a real obligation to show your father that things are different in your life now."

Hal Seybold started at the admonition. "You just don't know what he's like, Danny," he answered, a little irritated. "He doesn't want me to do anything. He'll keep me away from seeing you and going to church and everything."

Danny smiled. "I know, but the Bible says, 'Honor thy father and thy mother…' That means we must obey whether we like it or not."

Hal was incredulous. "Even if he tells me not to go to church?" he asked.

"We'll pray that he *will* let you go to church, Hal."

The Seybold boy fidgeted nervously, and it was a moment or two before anyone spoke.

Kay went to the refrigerator. "Sit down and have a glass of milk and some cookies, Hal."

"Boy, that sounds good. Dad got mad at me this morning when I didn't get up quickly. He wouldn't let me have any breakfast."

Hal drank the milk and hungrily ate the cookies. Danny Orlis waited until he had finished. "Did your dad tell you that you shouldn't come here?" he asked.

Hal colored and spoke hesitantly. "No – but I know he doesn't like you. I just figured he wouldn't let me come here."

He leaned forward and his voice rose defensively. "Now it doesn't make any difference where I want to go or what I want to do," he said. "If he knows I'd like it, he tries to stop me."

Danny was slow in replying, but when he did his words were deep and searching. "Are you trying to get along with your dad, Hal?" he demanded gently.

The boy's lower lip trembled. "Sure, but since I've become a Christian it's worse than before. The harder I try the worse it gets!"

The youthful face darkened. "I get so mad at him."

Danny smiled slightly, perhaps to soften his words. "Perhaps that's the trouble, Hal," he said. "You get mad at your dad and say things you shouldn't. He flies at you, and the first thing you know you are fighting."

"I try to keep from getting mad, Danny, but you just can't help it. I do everything I can to keep from having trouble with him. It doesn't do any good. He just keeps yelling and yelling until I lose my temper and tell him off!"

Young Orlis was gentle. "Have you ever tried praying for him, Hal?" he asked.

A strange look came on Hal's face. "Sure, I've prayed for him. I–I've even tried talking with him about the Lord Jesus, but that makes him madder."

"Just keep on praying for him, Hal," Danny said. "That's the answer. That's the only real answer. The Holy Spirit has to work in your dad's life before he'll accept Christ as his Saviour."

"Maybe you're right." Hal spoke doubtfully.

"I know I'm right. You pray for your dad. Pray that God will help you to speak kindly and understandingly to him. When he loses his temper, pray that you'll keep yours and not answer back."

A strange, hurt look crossed the boy's face. "I sure thought you'd see how it is. I didn't think you'd stick up for him."

"We don't stick up for him, Hal – believe me. Both Kay and I understand what a problem you have. We're praying for both of you regularly."

"What I really came to tell you," Hal said, "is that I won't be seeing you anymore, I guess." The boy's face was somber.

CHAPTER 2

JIM MEETS DOUG

Jim Morgan was late in getting home from school the afternoon Kay's letter arrived. Mrs. Wayman had propped it up on the table just inside the front door.

"There's a letter for you, Jim," she called from the kitchen.

He picked it up. "It's from Angle Inlet," he answered, "but it's not from the folks. It isn't Aunt Mary's handwriting."

He was staring at the short letter inside.

"Is it bad news?" Mrs. Wayman asked.

"Bad news?" Jim echoed. "I should say it isn't! In fact, this is just about the best news I've ever had!"

It still didn't seem possible. There had to be some mistake, but no, it didn't sound that way.

He went to the telephone and called Ron. "Ron! Guess what!"

"What? I'll guess," Ron said. "Simmer down a little, fella! You're about to blow a gasket!"

"You would be if you'd gotten this letter I have. Danny and Kay wrote me from Angle Inlet."

"I didn't even know they were at home," Ron said.

"Neither did anyone else. Danny's been transferred to Gluymon, Ontario, north of Kenora. He and Kay want me to transfer to the school up there and live with them this winter."

There was a short silence; then, "Lucky stiff." "I sure wish you could go with me," Jim said.

That night Jim Morgan thought he would never be able to go to sleep. Every time he closed his eyes, he could see Danny and Kay, or the little house at the Angle with Aunt Mary and Uncle Carl Orlis sitting in front of the fireplace.

Now he was going to spend the whole winter with Danny, and they'd be living close enough so they'd be able to get back to the Angle often. He prayed a prayer of thanksgiving before finally drifting off to sleep.

Ron and Roxie Orlis came to Cedarton from the Bible Institute the following morning and went to the school principal with Jim to tell of the coming transfer. Then they helped the boy get his bus ticket to Warroad.

"I can manage now, Ron," Jim said. "Thanks a lot."

"I'll help you get your bags packed, if you wish."

"I can take care of that, all right." Jim paused. "About the only reason I hate to leave is that I won't be able to see you and Roxie very often."

"You may see us more often than you think, Jim," Ron said. "We'll be back every chance we get."

The Orlis twins went to the bus with him. Roxie wanted to kiss him good-by. Jim felt like a fool for letting her do it, but he had to admit there wasn't anyone nicer than Roxie.

Danny had told him when to be in Warroad. He would be there to meet him. When the bus pulled in, there was Danny, just as he had said. A fellow about Jim's age was standing beside him.

"Hi, Danny!" Jim exclaimed, rushing off the bus.

"I see you made it."

"I said I'd be here, didn't I?"

"This is going to be great," Jim said. "When I read Kay's letter, I thought maybe she was kidding. I can hardly believe that it's true."

"It looks as though you're stuck with us," Danny told him. Then he remembered the boy who had ridden to Warroad from Gluymon with him. "I almost forgot to introduce you. Doug, Jim. Doug Ellis' dad works for the mine, too."

"Hi, I'm sure glad to meet you." Jim thrust out his hand.

Doug laughed cryptically.

The bus driver put Jim's suitcase on the curb. Jim picked it up and walked with Danny and Doug over to the car which Orlis had borrowed.

"Have they got a football team at Gluymon, Doug?" Jim asked.

"Yeah, but it wouldn't do you any good," Doug

countered. "Getting in late, you won't get to play. The positions are filled."

If Jim was disappointed, it did not show. "I probably wouldn't be good enough to make the junior high team, anyway," he said. "But believe me, I'm sure going out for hockey and basketball."

"I don't think you'd have a chance there." A sneer came to his thin lips. "They've got some real athletes in Gluymon. It's not like most towns."

Jim straightened slightly. "I suppose you play."

"A little." The smile came back to play with the corners of his mouth. "I'm the quarterback on our football team. I was high-scorer in both hockey and basketball last year at Tanbark. I do the kicking and passing for our team and make most of the long running gains. If the line just opens a hole I can do all right."

After clearing Customs, they flew on to Gluymon.

"I've been meaning to ask you, Danny," Jim said, "what's the church at Gluymon like? Do they have many young people?"

"Actually, we haven't been in town long enough to find out."

Doug broke in contemptuously then. "Let me clue you in, Jim. You don't have to have church when you're around Orlis. He preaches all the time."

Jim's face flushed. "And I can tell you that what Danny says is true. A fellow is a lot happier after he becomes a Christian."

Doug Ellis laughed again. "I might have known

you'd fall for that," he said scornfully. "You're just about the kind of a guy who would."

Jim did not argue.

When they landed at the lake near the little mining town, Danny put the plane in a hangar the company had built out over the water for him. Then they started for the little company house where Jim would be living with Danny and Kay.

"What do you think of Doug?" Danny Orlis asked when they were alone.

Jim was silent for a moment. "If you really want to know, he's a real foul ball."

"He's one of the boys we've been praying for since we've been here, Jim," Danny said. "We'd sure appreciate your prayers for him. He doesn't know the Lord, and he's terribly antagonistic toward everything that's Christian."

"I know exactly what he's like. He's just the way I used to be," Jim said.

They walked on for a hundred yards or so before either spoke.

"I'm afraid Doug is headed for trouble unless he is won to Christ," Danny went on. "He started doing some things up at Tanbark that could have gotten him into a real jam."

Danny slowed down. "Unfortunately, he's a leader. If he gets into trouble, the chances are he'll take several other fellows with him."

"I'll pray for him," Jim said. "You can count on me.

"And witness to him too," Danny urged. "We mustn't forget. Praying is important, but sometimes we use it as an easy way out."

He changed the subject abruptly. "There's another fellow here who's going to need your help too, Jim, and I think you can do him more good than anybody else."

"Who's that?" Jim asked. "Have you ever written about him?"

"I hardly think so. He's the fellow who was stranded with me when I was forced down north of Tanbark a few weeks ago."

"I remember. Didn't you tell me his name was Hal?"

Danny nodded. "Yes, Hal Seybold. He's a Christian now, but he hasn't known the Lord very long. He doesn't know much about how a Christian ought to live. The thing he needs is good Christian fellowship with someone like yourself, someone who knows something of separation and solid Christian living."

There was a wistful trace in Jim's voice when he spoke.

"That's something *I've* been praying about, Danny. Ever since I knew I'd be moving to Gluymon, I've been asking God for a friend here. I had a few Christian buddies in Cedarton and I wanted at least one here."

Hal Seybold was sitting in the house with Kay when Danny and Jim came in.

"I didn't expect to see you here, Hal," Danny said. "I thought you were still at Tanbark."

"I thought I was going to be stuck up there, all alone, too, but the mine transferred Dad down here to work."

"Fine," Danny said and introduced him to Jim.

"I'm sure glad to meet you," Hal said. "I've been anxious to meet you since Danny and Kay told me you were coming."

Jim Morgan smiled warmly and thrust out his hand. "Glad to know you, too. It's going to be good to have a Christian buddy."

A strange look came into Hal's face. "I wouldn't know," he retorted. "I've never had one."

* * *

Hal came by the next morning, and he and Jim walked to school together. Doug Ellis met them at the front door.

"I see you two guys got together. What are you going to do, have a prayer meeting?"

Before either could reply, Doug went inside laughing.

The color came to Hal's face. "Sometime he's going to make a crack like that and I'm going to pop him," Hal said. "I'm not going to take it!"

Jim glanced at him. "Don't get so shook up. He just makes cracks like that because he thinks it will make us mad. When he finds out it doesn't, he'll quit."

Doug had been right about the school not allowing Jim to go for football.

However, when Mr. Elliot, the coach, learned that Jim was staying at Danny's he was interested in meeting him. "You know, Jim," the coach said, "I used to play football against Danny when we were in high school together. I've never seen anyone play football like he did."

"Ron said Danny was pretty good."

"Good?" Elliot exclaimed. "He was the best player I ever played against – in either high school or college. If he'd really wanted to, he could have gone professional and made a big name for himself. He was a tremendous quarterback."

Jim's face twisted into a grin.

"Do you think Danny is home now?" Elliot asked.

"He ought to be back by five o'clock. He usually is."

"I'm going over to see him. I'd sure like to have him help me with this football team."

That night Bill Elliot stopped to see Danny Orlis.

"It's sure good to see you, Bill. I don't believe I've seen you since we played college football," Danny said.

"That's right."

Danny introduced Elliot to Kay. "I didn't even know you were in this town, Bill. How long have you been around?"

"My wife and I moved here in August before school started," Elliot replied.

Danny smiled. "You've been here a little longer than we have," he replied. "We came from Tanbark. I'm flying for the mine."

"That's what Jim says."

Bill smiled. "That was a surprise. The way you always talked religion, I figured you'd wind up being a preacher."

"We started out that way," Danny answered easily, "but the Lord had other plans for us."

A question showed in his visitor's eyes.

"Kay and I were on the mission field in Guatemala for a while, but we had to come back."

Kay, sitting across from Elliot, looked up. Disappointment showed in her eyes.

Bill Elliot leaned back in the chair and crossed his legs. "When I used to play football against you, Danny, I sure didn't figure we would be living up here together," he said. "I always thought you should have gone to a good football university for pro ball after graduation. You had it, Danny. You could have knocked down big money and not have had to work hard, either."

Danny ran a finger along his chin thoughtfully. "I guess the idea was as tempting to me as it is to a lot of fellows," he said, "but I can tell you honestly that I've never been sorry for the choices Kay and I have made."

"No, I suppose you haven't."

"We'll probably never have much money, but Kay and I both feel we're in the Lord's will. That, to us, is most important."

Bill squirmed a little. "Well, I'm glad you're here, Danny, whatever your reason. I could use you for the next month or so, if you'd be willing to help me."

"Sure thing. In any way I can."

The youthful coach brightened. "I've got some good fast boys in the backfield, but they need a little help in mastering some of the things you used to do when you were running over us guys in the fine."

"I haven't had a football in my hands in years," Danny said, "but I'll do what I can."

"That'll be plenty."

CHAPTER 3

GAME SUMMED UP, GORDY BLAKE

Danny Orlis finished work a little earlier than usual the next morning, and that afternoon by the time football practice began he was on hand at the school. Bill Elliot introduced him to the fellows and told them why he was there.

Danny gave them a short lecture on ball handling and broken field running. Then he turned back to the coach.

"Why don't you have them run off a few plays, Bill? That'll give an idea of what the fellows can do."

"I was about to suggest that. Watch Gordy Blake. He's the best ballcarrier we've got."

Danny Orlis stood on the sidelines near the coach and watched while they ran off four or five plays.

"Think you've seen enough?" Elliot asked.

Danny nodded. "Gordy is good. He's got real possibilities."

The coach blew his whistle and called the fellows together.

"Gordy, you're fast and shifty," Danny said appraisingly, "but you're giving away a good share of the advantage your speed gives you?"

The halfback frowned. "What do you mean?"

"Coach Elliot has worked out some good, deceptive plays. As you know, they're designed to conceal the location of the ball from the tacklers as long as possible. But on plays on which you have been doing the carrying, you've given yourself away."

Gordy broke in belligerently. "Now how do you figure that?"

"Just before the ball is snapped on your plays, you wipe your hands on your trousers," Danny told him. "An alert defensive man will catch that and smear you before you get started."

"I'm the best ground gainer on the team I think," Gordy protested.

"I know that. But if you can whip this thing, you'll be able to do even better."

While Coach Elliot worked with the rest of the squad, Danny took Gordy Blake and a center off to one side and began to work with them. He showed Gordy how to stand so it would look as though he were going to carry the ball on every play – how to increase the deception as the plays got under way, and little tricks to throw the tacklers off guard.

"The best ballcarriers have little tricks like these to help them gain another yard or two."

"I'd never thought of it quite that way."

After an hour of work with Gordy, Danny returned to the squad.

He spoke softly to Bill Elliot. "That boy's really got it. I'm anxious to see what he can do against opposition."

Gordy Blake took the ball on the first play, faked it to the fullback who came up fast, turned sharply and knifed through tackle. The second team was caught off guard by the speed of the play, and he blasted through for twenty-seven yards before he was forced out of bounds.

Two plays later he snapped around end, dodged a defensive back and plunged across for a touchdown.

Coach Elliot was jubilant. "That's it, Gordy! Now, you're rolling."

Word of Danny Orlis' help on the football field spread rapidly around the school. Jim heard it and came home excited. "Boy, you're really the big hero out at school these days, Danny," he said. "The guys are all talking about what you did for Gordy Blake. They say you're going to help us plow right through the remaining games."

"I can teach them a few tricks," Danny Orlis replied, "but they've got to master the fundamentals Coach Elliot is teaching and learn to snap off the plays. They'll have to win their own ball games."

Kay came to the kitchen door and called them to dinner. "Do you think you two can leave football long enough to come in and eat?"

"Just try us and see," Danny countered.

While eating he turned to Jim Morgan. "How are you coming with Hal, Jim?"

"Oh, he's a great guy. As good a friend as I've ever had, and I've only known him a little while."

"That's not exactly what I mean," he said. "How is he doing spiritually?"

Jim hesitated a moment. "To tell the truth, Danny, I don't get much of a chance to talk with Hal about spiritual things."

"What do you mean?" Kay asked.

"It's that Doug Ellis. He's hanging around with Hal all the time. Won't leave him alone for a minute. Every time I try to talk with Hal about Christian living, Doug's got some wise remark that freezes Hal – but good."

Danny pursed his lips. "That's bad."

"As far as I can figure, Doug's doing a good job of holding Hal back," Jim continued.

Kay's face grew thoughtful. "Isn't that a terrible thing? It's bad enough when a person like Doug won't listen to spiritual things, but when he'll deliberately try to hold back someone else it's even worse."

Danny smiled and rumpled Jim's hair. "You keep on the job, fella."

Danny Orlis continued to work with the football team all that week. While Coach Elliot handled the squad, Danny spent a night with each of the backs, showing them painstakingly how to run and handle the ball. However, it seemed that only Gordy Blake was able to gain real help from the pointers. All week long the fleet halfback ran roughshod over the second team.

"I think you've got yourself a good football player in Gordy," Danny said. "If he can go against Black Water the way he has against the second team, you ought to beat them easily."

The day of the game came, and Black Water kicked off to Gluymon. The first play was set up on the eighteen-yard line. Coach Elliot, who had asked Danny to sit on the bench with him, punched him in the side.

"They've called for an off-tackle smash with Gordy carrying the ball."

Gordy took the pigskin in a hand-off from the quarterback, faded to his left as though to pass or give it to the other half, and exploded over tackle.

The line opened a hole and he went blasting out into the open. He eluded two tacklers and a third by reversing his field, and scampered to the fifty-yard line before being forced out of bounds.

They called the same play a second time and he drove through to the twenty-one yard line. The powerful Black Water eleven called time out.

"I told you that you had yourself a ball player," Danny said.

"I've got to give you credit. He didn't run that way before you took hold of him, Danny."

The rest of the ball game could have been summed up in a name, Gordy Blake. The fleet-footed halfback ran over, around, and through the Black Water defense. And when the final gun sounded, Gluymon had beaten the team they were supposed to lose to by the score of 28-0.

CHAPTER 4

DANNY AND KAY SPONSOR YOUNG PEOPLE'S

The following Monday afternoon when Danny came into the locker room to change into his football uniform for practice, Gordy Blake was sitting waiting for him.

"Hi, Gordy," Danny said warmly.

"Hello, Mr. Orlis."

As Danny took off his shoes, Gordy stepped closer. "I want to thank you for all the things you showed me last week. I never would have been able to make those runs if it hadn't been for you."

"If you didn't have what it takes, the things I showed you wouldn't have done you much good," Danny answered.

Gordy shifted from one foot to the other. "I–I don't mind telling you I was sort of teed off at you when you told me I was giving away my plays. But you were right. After I got to thinking about it, I realized I was doing just that."

The young pilot reached out and rumpled his hair affectionately. Danny finished dressing; then he and the star halfback went out to the practice field together. Jim Morgan was standing nearby. When he saw Danny, he came over.

"Hi, Danny," he said. "May I see you for a second?"

"Sure thing." He turned to Gordy. "I'll be right back."

Gordy went on to the football field, and Danny stopped beside the Morgan boy. "What's on your mind?" he asked.

"Some of the fellows on the junior high team were asking me if I could get you to come over and give them pointers too. They'd ask, but they're scared."

"I'm helping Coach Elliot tonight," Danny replied, "so I won't be able to."

He thought for a moment while disappointment flickered in Jim's eyes. "I don't believe I'll be flying anywhere this Saturday, Jim. If it's all right with their coach, and if they want to get together in that vacant lot across from our place, I'll do what I can to help them then."

Jim grinned broadly. "Thanks, Danny. Thanks a lot. I told the fellows you'd help. I knew you would."

There was another high school game that Friday night. Gordy Blake was held to one touchdown and two long runs, but in spite of that Gluymon won handily.

"We won another one, Danny," the coach said.

"You've been just the spark we've needed to get our fellows to have confidence in themselves and their ability."

Saturday morning was cold and frosty, but when ten o'clock came there were almost a dozen fellows in Danny's backyard waiting for him. He worked with them until noon, showing them some of the things he had taught the varsity.

Shortly after twelve o'clock, Kay called Danny and Jim to dinner.

"Thanks, Danny," the fellows called. "Thanks a lot."

He waved to them. "Come over any time when I'm not busy. I'll be glad to help you."

Jim opened the door, and he and the young pilot went inside. "That was awesome, Danny," he said. "The guys really appreciated it, and so did I. I didn't know there was so much to learn about football."

"There's a lot to learn if you're going to do a decent job of playing the game, and you've got to be willing to work hard."

They finished eating and were still sitting at the table when Rev. Carl Grant came to the door. He was an intense individual, some twelve or fifteen years older than Danny, and becoming gray.

"I've been wanting to visit you and your wife ever since you moved in," the minister said, "but somehow time hasn't permitted."

"We're certainly glad you stopped," Danny replied.

They went into the living room and sat down.

"I haven't had a chance to become acquainted with

you and Mrs. Orlis," Mr. Grant continued, "but I've heard a great deal about you."

"I hope it's been good," Danny told him.

Mr. Grant nodded. "You know it has been. Very much so."

For a moment or two he paused. "My wife and I came up here to Gluymon because of the challenge the work presents. The church is new, you know, but it is beginning to grow."

"We were aware of that. Kay and I were talking this morning about the way the Sunday school attendance is picking up. We were going by the figures on the attendance board."

"There have been many things in the work here to encourage us," Rev. Grant said. "But there is something we've been praying about. We need a young people's society. But we haven't been able to start one because there hasn't been a person capable enough to organize it."

Danny and Kay glanced at one another.

"Last night the church board met and unanimously voted to ask you and Mrs. Orlis to take over sponsorship of the young people. May we count on you?"

There was a short silence. "We want to help all we can," Danny said. "Do you think Kay and I could do a good job for you?"

"We're convinced of it. My wife and I have been praying about this for weeks. Every time we start considering prospective leaders, we come back to you. Several members of the board said they had had the same experience."

Neither Danny nor Kay answered immediately.

"If you'd like to think it over and pray about it, you may give us your answer later."

"We have been praying about an avenue of service here, Mr. Grant," Danny replied. "I don't think it's necessary to wait about giving our answer, do you, Kay?"

She shook her head. "We've always enjoyed working with young people," Kay added.

The pastor beamed his pleasure. "I had no idea you'd give your answer today. It's a real encouragement for a pastor when people will respond quickly. We'll be seeing you again to work out the details."

The announcement was made in church the next day, and, according to Jim, it spread rapidly over the school.

"Boy, Danny, everybody wants to come to young people's now that they know you're going to be there. You sure have made a name for yourself by helping Gordy Blake."

"It would be better if they would come to young people's because they wanted to know Jesus Christ better rather than because of me. I might let them down some day. He never will."

The first young people's meeting was held the following Thursday, and twenty-eight fellows and girls came out. Danny and Kay were greatly encouraged.

They locked the church and walked home together in the chill October air.

"Wasn't that a good beginning, Danny?" Kay asked.

"As good as we could possibly hope for," he said.

"I don't imagine that more than two or three of them really know the Lord Jesus as Saviour, but they certainly were attentive when you were talking. I think they are as eager about getting organized as any group I've ever seen."

Danny nodded. "They were that, all right. But to tell you the truth, Kay, I was a little disappointed. I thought Doug Ellis might be there."

Jim came running up just then. "Hey, wait for me!

They stopped and waited until he came up to them. "What did you think of the meeting tonight, Jim?"

"It was super."

"Doug Ellis didn't come," Danny added.

"Hal told me he was going to work on Doug," Kay said, "to see if he could get him to start coming."

Jim nodded. "That's right. Doug tried his best to talk Hal out of going at all. He kept telling him he'd have to give up everything that was any fun if he kept getting into stuff at church."

"What did Hal have to say to that?" Danny asked.

"He didn't say much of anything. Doug was the one who did all the talking. He said the pastor wouldn't let Hal go to shows or do anything he wanted to. All he'd be able to do would be to sit around and read the Bible."

Danny Orlis smiled. "That's one thing people who aren't Christian can never understand. They think that once a person accepts Christ, he never has a good time again. They don't realize that God will take away old desires and give new things to enjoy."

They walked on for half a block or more before Jim continued. "When I was thinking about this whole business of becoming a Christian, that was what threw me more than anything else. I figured a Christian couldn't do anything that was fun, and I wanted to have a good time. I didn't realize how wrong I was until after I had accepted Christ."

A few nights after the first young people's meeting Doug Ellis came over to Hal's to get him to go to the library with him. Big Ed, Hal's father, was home, sober, but surly and short-tempered.

"Where do you think you're going?" he demanded.

"Out," Hal spoke curtly.

"Don't get smart with me. I can see you're going out. What I want to know is where you're going."

"Doug and I have got some things to do."

"You answer me, Hal Seybold, or you'll be sorry you didn't! I suppose you're going to that church again. That seems to be where you spend most of your time these days. Over there, or with that stupid Orlis!"

"No," he retorted, "we're not going over to the church!" His voice rose. "And we're not going over to Danny's either. I don't know why you've been so concerned lately as to where I'm going and what I'm doing. You never cared before."

Big Ed was loud and belligerent. "Don't give me any more of your lip, young man, or I'll make you wish you hadn't."

Doug Ellis got to his feet uneasily and started toward the door. "I've got to be going, Hal."

Hal turned to his dad.

"Are you through lecturing to me? Or can I go now?" His lips curled in bitterness.

Doug Ellis fled.

Big Ed took a step toward the boy, menacingly. "Now I'll teach you some manners!"

CHAPTER 5

A GREAT FIELD OF SERVICE

Miserably, Hal Seybold went in and went to bed. What was the matter with him and his dad, anyway? Why couldn't they be like other people? Why did they have to keep fighting?

He slipped out of bed and knelt to pray. "Dear God, help Dad and me to get along better and not to fight all the time. Help him to keep from drinking and to take Jesus as his Savior…."

The next morning when he got up, his father was just going out the door. "I see you finally got up." There was an edge to Big Ed's voice.

Hal started to retort hotly but stopped.

"See that you're home by the time I get back," his dad snarled. "D'you hear?"

"I'll be here." He got a bowl from the cupboard and took some cereal. Dad never seemed satisfied unless he was in a bad mood. Why didn't he want to get along?

Doug Ellis was waiting for Hal on the comer near his home to walk to school with him. "I'll bet you really got it last night after I left," Doug said.

"It wasn't so bad."

"Boy, was your old man teed off last night!"

"That was just normal," Hal said.

"All we were going to do was go to the library," Doug continued. "He didn't have any reason to lip off that way."

"Don't I know it!"

Doug's face darkened. "I wouldn't stand for it if I were you!"

Hal stopped. "Just what would you do about it if you were me?" he asked. "That's the way he's always treated me, especially since I became a Christian."

As Hal talked about his father, his temper grew. When he got to school, he was so upset and angry besides feeling so sorry for himself that it was all he could think about. He almost flunked a history test that morning.

* * *

Danny Orlis continued to help Coach Elliot work with Gordy Blake and the rest of the backfield. In addition, he and the coach got together and worked out a series of new plays to take advantage of the increased ball-handling ability of the backs.

"I would have tried to do this before," Bill Elliot told the squad as he outlined the plays on the board, "but until you could handle the ball well and had mastered some of the things Danny has been showing you, it wouldn't have done any good."

They learned the new plays and practiced them until they came off with clockwork precision. Still, they didn't use them in a game. Gordy couldn't understand it.

"When are we going to give those plays a try, Coach?" he asked.

Bill Elliot laughed. "When we meet Royal," he said. "We'll have something new to throw at them – something they've never seen before."

* * *

The young people's work was moving along equally well. The number in attendance grew from week to week as more of the students came out. Even Gordy Blake showed up one night with his girlfriend.

Hal leaned over and nudged Jim Morgan. "Look who just came in. He's one guy I sure didn't figure on seeing in church."

Jim nodded. "He's a real friend of Danny's now."

When the meeting was over, Gordy came to Danny and introduced his girlfriend, Joyce Carrigan.

"That was a great meeting, Mr. Orlis," Gordy told him. "I think we'll be coming back."

Danny called Kay over and introduced her. "Why don't you drop by the house sometime?" Kay asked.

A peculiar look crossed Gordy's face. "Do you mean it?"

"Certainly we mean it," Danny put in. "We'd like to have you."

There was a short silence. "Thank you," Joyce said, smiling. "That sounds like fun."

Gordy Blake turned to go. "We might take you up on that sometime, Mrs. Orlis. Thanks, a lot."

Hal Seybold came to young people's regularly, in spite of the way his dad felt. Big Ed didn't tell him he couldn't go, but he stormed about it whenever he knew Hal had been to a meeting at church or had stopped to visit Danny and Kay.

"I don't know why you waste your time going to that church," he snorted. "Nobody ever got any good out of it!"

"How would you know? You've never been there!"

"I don't have to go to know that. It sure hasn't done you any good. You're still as mouthy as ever!"

Hal went over to talk with Kay about the situation. "I just don't know what to do, Kay," he confided. "It's getting worse. It used to be that he'd give me a little rest, especially when he was sober. Now he's after me all the time. And especially if I go to church, young people's or come over to see you and Danny."

There was a brief silence. "How do you treat him?" she asked.

Hal hesitated. "I want to treat him right," he said defensively, "but he keeps after me and after me until I just can't help myself."

Kay Orlis sat down across from him. She spoke gently. "You're a Christian now, Hal. Your father and all the people around you who aren't Christians are going to be watching everything you do. If you show your dad that you have something different than he has, he's going to become interested in being a Christian. But if you don't – if you lose your temper the same as he does and talk back to him the way you used to, it's going to be hard for you to witness effectively to him."

Hal sat still for a long while. "I–I really haven't been the way I should be," he told her. "I know that."

"Have you ever told him that?"

He shook his head.

"Have you prayed about it?" she continued. "Have you asked God to forgive you?"

"I've done that. Lots of times," he said. "But going to Dad – that's different."

"The Bible tells us that we should get straightened out with the person we've wronged. We are to come to God and ask Him to forgive us."

They prayed together before Hal went home. His heart was hammering fiercely as he entered the house.

"Is that you, Hal?" Big Ed snapped. "Where've you been?"

Hal hung up his coat and went into the living room where his father was sprawled on a chair. "Over talking to Mrs. Orlis."

Big Ed snorted. "Thought I told you to steer clear of that outfit."

"You didn't say I couldn't go over and see them," Hal reminded him.

"I told you what I think of them. That ought to be enough to keep you away from there, if you were any kind of a son at all."

The Seybold boy stared at his father. At first, he thought his dad had been drinking again; on closer inspection he saw that he hadn't. At least his face didn't carry the unnatural flush that usually came over it when he had been drinking.

Hal took a deep breath. "Dad, I–I want to tell you I'm sorry I lost my temper all the times I've talked to you."

Big Ed stared at him suspiciously. "Now what are you up to?"

"Why–" Hal replied, startled a little by the accusation in his dad's voice, "I did something wrong and I want to apologize. Honest, I'm sorry. Really, I am."

Big Ed Seybold straightened in his chair. "That Orlis dame put you up to it, didn't she?"

For a moment Hal did not answer.

"Didn't she?"

"We talked about the way I've been treating you," Hal admitted.

"That's just some more of their lousy tricks. Want to make me think they're such wonderful people. They're trying to soft-soap me for something. But I can tell you this much, it's not going to work. I'm on to their kind. I'm not falling for that!"

Hal stared at him in amazement.

* * *

That night when Danny came in from flying up to Tanbark with supplies, he found Kay quiet and pensive. "What's the matter, Kay?" he said. "You don't seem to be yourself."

"I'm all right."

He put his hand on her shoulder and gently turned her to face him. "You never were any good at hiding your feelings," he said. "What's wrong?"

She went over and sat down, wearily. "Nothing, Danny. Really. It's just that–"

"What is it, Kay?"

She shrugged in a quick, nervous gesture. "I suppose it sounds silly, but I've been concerned about something all day."

"I knew there was something."

"I've been asking myself just what I've been doing for the Lord. When have I been helping to advance His kingdom? To whom have I been able to witness?"

Danny smiled. He went over and sat down beside her. "Kay," he said quietly, "I want you to think back over this week. Have you had anybody here?"

"A few."

"How many?" he insisted.

"Oh, I don't know, Danny. Really, I don't. I suppose there have been ten or twelve. Mostly young people."

"I thought so. How many of them came because they had some problem they wanted to talk over with you – because they knew you are sympathetic and wouldn't be shocked by what they told you?"

She thought for a moment. "I guess three or four had some things they wanted to talk over," she said. "I don't know that I was really able to help them."

"You know, Kay, there's a tremendous ministry in having an open door of Christian kindness and friendliness. Did you ever think of that? I think God is opening a great field of service to you – a great field of service to us both."

CHAPTER 6

HAL HADN'T PLANNED IT AT ALL

The football team breezed through the remaining games until the final contest with Royal. Coach Elliot called the squad to order before taking them onto the field.

"This is not just another football game, fellows," he told them seriously. "This is for the conference championship. You can win it if you really put in everything you've got. But it's going to take everything!"

Determination glinted in their eyes and tightened their lips.

"But you're going to have to play harder than you've played before. That's one thing for sure. Get out there and show them how to play the game."

Danny Orlis stood beside the football coach at the edge of the field. Bill Elliot turned to him before the start of the game. "Think we can do it?"

"What did you just tell the boys?" Danny asked.

He laughed in answer. "I sure don't know why I ever went into this business in the first place. Why didn't I go into something nice and easy like testing space capsules or chasing mountain goats?"

"If those kids of ours play the way we know they can, there isn't another school of our size anywhere in the state that can beat us," Danny reminded him.

"I sure hope you're right."

Royal won the toss and chose to receive. Gluymon stopped them cold after three plays, took a long punt on their own thirty-yard line, and started to march down the field. Gordy carried the ball on the first two plays but was stopped cold.

Danny looked over at Bill. "They're rushing Gordy every time the ball is snapped, Bill," he said. "They aren't even trying to figure out the plays."

The coach nodded. "They probably think they've got us stopped if they can stop him."

Elliot turned as though to send in a substitute but waited for another play.

This time Gordy crouched as though to take the ball. However, he stepped aside as it was snapped and let it go to the fullback. The line swarmed in to nail the Gluymon speedster behind the line of scrimmage, but the fullback blasted over the guard for a fourteen-yard gain.

"Now that wasn't such bad thinking," Danny Orlis said. The tightness in the coach's face relaxed a little.

"That's just the way you used to do when we tried to clobber you before you got under way, Danny."

Danny grinned, remembering.

The game was hard fought all the way, but there was never any doubt as to the outcome. The broken field running of Gordy Blake spelled the difference. When the final whistle sounded, Gluymon had defeated Royal by two touchdowns.

In the locker room Bill Elliot told the fellows how proud he was of them. "Gordy made the long runs, but you fellows all know that if it hadn't been for the line and the rest of the backfield playing a bang-up game all the way, Gordy wouldn't have been able to get up to the line of scrimmage."

"That's right," the fleet-footed back said. "The line opened up holes for me. All I did was to run through them."

"Just wait until next fall," one of the players said exultantly. "We'll have Gordy Blake and most of the line in school again. Just wait until next year. We'll really clobber everybody."

At school the next day excitement ran high. Everyone was talking about a victory celebration the businessmen in town had promised.

Hal told Jim all about it. "They want to give the whole school something to show them how much the town appreciates the hard work the team put in and the way all the kids stood behind them."

"I thought that big trophy we won was enough," Jim said. "Did you see that thing? It's a foot high."

"I know," Hal went on, "but this celebration is going to be something, too. We're going to get out of school a whole day just to take part in everything."

"Sounds great to me. Especially that getting out of school business."

Doug Elks came up just then and heard what they were talking about. "You guys won't be able to enjoy it anyway," he said. "I don't know why you're so excited about it."

Jim snorted good-naturedly. "Don't fool yourself. We'll have as much fun as anyone else."

Doug laughed. "Maybe you will at that. They're having a big dance for the senior high kids, and do you know what they're having for us? A free football picture at the theater! The mine superintendent is bringing it in free to show it."

"That doesn't interest me," Jim said. "I gave up that stuff a long time ago."

Doug grinned. "The trouble is that you don't know any better. That's all."

Hal and Doug left Jim Morgan and went off in the direction of their homes. They had walked a block or more before Doug spoke. "You're not going to let that dopey Jim Morgan keep you from going to an awesome free show, are you?" he asked.

"I'm not going to let him keep me from going," Hal answered.

A strange, relieved look came to Doug's face. "I knew you wouldn't," he replied, his voice warmer and more friendly than it had been for weeks.

"It's not Jim Morgan who's going to keep me from going. I don't want to go myself."

Doug stopped and grasped him by the arm. "Now wait a minute. You can't give me that stuff. You're as crazy about shows as I am. You can't fool me."

There was a brief silence. "Remember all those good westerns we used to see when we lived at Tanbark?"

Hal did not answer.

"And this one's free," Doug continued. "That's the best part…. You've just got to go with me, Hal. You can't turn me down!"

"It's not going to do you any good to talk," Hal replied. "I won't be going to the show."

"Of all the goofy ideas!" Doug snorted. "You try to tell me it's so wonderful to be a Christian, but look how you are about a little thing like going to a show. No sir, I don't want any of that stuff! I'm going to have fun!"

Hal picked up a stone and chucked it along the street. "That's because you don't know what it's like to be a Christian," he answered. "Why don't you go to young people's with me, Doug? Then you'll see what good times we have without dancing and going to shows."

Doug Ellis turned toward him suddenly. "I'll tell you what I'll do. You go with me to this football picture, and I'll go with you to young people's. How's that for a deal?"

Hal hesitated uncertainly.

"Or do you have to ask Danny Orlis first to see if it's all right?" Doug demanded disdainfully.

Hal took a deep breath. "Will you go to young people's with me before the show?"

"Sure I will," Doug agreed. "Only you've got to give me your word of honor that you'll go to the show with me. That's the only way I'll ever go to church with you."

Hal Seybold did not agree.

"Or are you too 'chicken' to do that?" Doug taunted.

"If you'll go to young people's with me," Hal said, making his decision with a suddenness that surprised himself, "I'll do it."

"Swell! You've got yourself a deal! And I can tell you this much. You'll never be sorry you've made it."

Hal was to have charge of the program the night Doug promised to attend. He was very concerned that he include just the right Scripture in his attempt to present the plan of salvation, so he went over to ask Kay to help him prepare.

"Doug has promised to go with me that night," he said. "The meeting is really important."

"That is good news, Hal. Danny, Jim and I will be praying that he'll be touched and accept the Gospel."

She paused. "I'm curious as to how you were able to get Doug to agree to go to young people's, Hal," she said at last. "He's been so opposed to meetings or anything Christian."

The boy's cheeks colored. "Oh, he and I made a little deal."

The next afternoon before the young people's meeting, Big Ed Seybold came into the bedroom where Hal was going over the program he was to lead.

"I thought I told you to get the storm windows on, Hal," Big Ed snorted belligerently.

Hal fought against anger that surged within him. "I've been awful busy, Dad," he tried to explain. "I'll do it tomorrow night right after school."

"No, you won't. You'll go right out now and get those storm windows put on. I've been after you to do it for a month. You aren't going to put it off again."

"But Dad!" Hal protested.

"I don't want to hear any more excuses. Do as you're told and be quick about it."

Hal put his Bible away and went to work. There wasn't a chance of getting those windows on before time to go to young people's! And he had to be there! Especially tonight with Doug coming and himself leading the meeting. They were depending on him.

He knew why it was that his dad had laid down the law about those storm windows. His father knew it was the night for young people's, and he was going to keep Hal away from church if he could. That was the only reason he got in such a sweat about those storm windows. He hadn't said a thing about putting them on the day before, or the day before that.

It wasn't fair. It wasn't fair at all! Hal ate supper as

quickly as he could and went back to the storm windows. It was a bigger job than he thought it was, and he was still working rapidly when Doug Ellis came by.

"Hi, are you ready to go?"

Hal looked up without stopping. "I'll be with you in a minute."

"It's getting late." Doug glanced at his watch. "We'd better be getting a move on."

Hal finished putting on the storm window he had been working on and went into the house for a clean shirt.

Big Ed heard him and came into the bedroom. "Now where do you think you're going?" he demanded. There was arrogance and anger in his voice.

Hal unbuttoned his shirt. "I–I've got to go over to church tonight, Dad," he stammered. "I'm leading the young people's meeting."

Big Ed eyed him suspiciously. "Get those storm windows up?"

There was a moment or two of hesitation. "Did you?" his father demanded. "Answer me or I'll clout you one!"

The Seybold boy had not intended to tell his dad something that wasn't true. He hadn't planned that at all. He had planned on leaving quietly, but the words popped out, unbidden.

"Sure, they're up."

Big Ed stared at him incredulously. Then he noisily got to his feet and followed Hal to the door.

"If you got those storm windows up," he blustered, "that's the fastest they have ever been put on. I'm going out and have a look."

Hal followed him around the house, numbly. At first his dad said nothing. When he turned to face Hal moments later, his face was livid. "You lied to me!" he roared. "A lot of good all that church going does you. You lied to me! Now get back into the house. You're not going anywhere!"

CHAPTER 7

THERE IS A WAY TO HELP

Hal Seybold stared in bewilderment at his dad. Perspiration sprinkled his forehead and he felt his face flush hotly. "I–I'm sorry. Dad. Honestly, I am. I–I didn't mean to tell you something that wasn't true. I–"

Big Ed laughed mirthlessly. "I'll say you didn't!" he snarled. "You didn't want to lie to me – at least that's what you're trying to tell me. But you did lie!"

He drew himself up to his full height, triumphantly, "And when do you apologize? When you get caught, that's when. You're no different than anyone else. That shows what that religion of yours actually amounts to!"

He took a step or two toward Hal. Involuntarily the boy cringed. "Now get the rest of those storm windows on and be quick about it! If they aren't on the house tonight, I'll give you a good thrashing! That's a promise!"

Hal looked at his father helplessly. "But Dad," he protested. "I don't have time to put the storm windows on. I–I've got to lead the young people's meeting over at church. I–I gave them my word!"

"You gave me your word that you'd put the storm windows on," Big Ed countered. "Now get at it, and let's not have any more back talk!"

Doug Ellis stood smirking, until Big Ed Seybold went back into the house. Then he turned on Hal. "Sounds like you're putting on the storm windows, the way I hear it."

Hal thrust his hands in his pocket and kicked disgustedly at a stone near the walk.

"Well, I'm waiting," Doug continued. "Are you going to the meeting with me, or aren't you?"

Hal's face was white and drawn and his lips trembling. "I–I guess I won't be able to go with you tonight, after all," he said at last. "I've got to stay and get those storm windows put on."

Doug laughed. "I came over to go to the meeting with you. That is, if you want me to."

Hal's gaze raised to meet Doug's. "If I want you?" he echoed. "I've been wanting you to go to young people's with me ever since we got it started."

The Ellis boy glanced at his watch. "Come on, then. It's going to be over before we get there if we don't get to moving."

Hal's lower lip trembled.

"You heard what Dad said. I've got to stay and work. I can't go tonight."

"Don't let a little thing like your old man bother you," Doug answered. "Just go ahead and lie to him the way you did about the storm windows. You won't be so unlucky twice in a row. You'll get away with it the second time."

Hal swallowed hard and rubbed his tightening throat. What could he say? Doug had heard him lie to his dad. He was probably thinking the same as his dad was, that being a Christian didn't make any difference in a fellow's life.

"How about going to the next young people's meeting with me?" Hal asked. "Will you go with me?"

Doug Ellis frowned. "I promised to go tonight, remember? And that's what I'm ready to do. I may not call myself a Christian, but I keep my word."

He turned deliberately and went swaggering away. Hal watched him miserably as Doug left.

The Seybold boy wanted to call Danny and Kay, but they had already gone to the church by the time he got to the telephone. He didn't get a chance to tell them that he wouldn't be able to take charge of the meeting. Dejectedly, he set to his work trying to put what had happened out of his mind.

Next evening after school he stopped at the Orlis home. Danny had just gotten in.

"I'm awfully sorry about last night," he said, "but I just couldn't make it."

Danny came in from the kitchen and looked at him. "Sometimes things do come up to make it impossible for us to get to meetings, I know," he said, his voice kindly. "It would have been better if you had told us in time for another program to be arranged."

Hal nodded miserably.

A faint smile softened the sting of Danny's words. "As it happened," Danny explained, "Kay and I were both at the meeting and were able to take over. But it doesn't always happen that way. Nothing will kill a young people's group quicker than dull programs – or no programs at all."

"I would have come if Dad had let me," Hal said, apologizing. "I was all ready to leave the house when he told me I couldn't go. There wasn't a thing I could do about it."

The boy sat down in an easy chair and Danny sat across from him.

For several moments Danny said nothing. Hal had something on his mind that was apparent. It was something that was bothering him a great deal. However, it seemed better to wait until he was ready to talk.

"The thing that makes it so bad," Hal continued at last, "is that I had finally talked Doug Ellis into going to young people's. Then, when Doug came over and we were ready to leave for the church, Dad wouldn't let me go."

His youthful voice rose. "He made me stay home and put up the storm windows! It seems as though Dad just waits until there's something going on at church before he makes me do something like that.

I think he does it just for spite – to keep me from getting to young people's or church."

Danny Orlis crossed his legs. "It's a little late to be putting on storm windows this far north, Hal," he said thoughtfully. "Hadn't your dad ever mentioned it to you before?"

Hal straightened and a queer, bewildered look flickered in his eyes. "Oh, I guess he had talked about it a few times," he answered defensively, "but he had never told me that I had to get it done until last night."

"You know, Hal," the young pilot said, "if you had gotten after them when your dad first told you to put them on, this wouldn't have happened."

The boy gulped, and it was a moment or two before he could speak.

"I–I guess you're right, but–" He chewed nervously on his lower lip. "I don't know what's wrong with me, Danny. It seems as though I never do the things I want to do."

Once he started to speak, the words came gushing out in a torrent. "I try to live a good Christian life and have been trying ever since I was saved. I even try to hold my temper when Dad starts giving me fits about something. But it seems as though I keep getting madder and madder at him until I can't keep from spouting off."

Danny listened patiently without comment.

"And then last night," Hal went on, "when Dad asked me if I had finished putting on the storm windows, I–I told him that I had, but I hadn't."

There was a long silence. "I could hardly sleep last night. But I finally confessed my sin to the Lord."

"That is fine, Hal," Danny said. "We all do things we shouldn't do. There's no doubt that you did wrong when you lied to your dad. You recognize that."

Hal nodded miserably.

"You've done the most important thing. You've asked God's forgiveness." Danny took a deep breath. "But you sinned against your father too. Have you asked him to forgive you?"

"I tried to, Danny. I felt terrible about it, and I told him I was sorry I had lied to him. But he said I apologized because I got caught."

His eyes grew big and luminous. "To tell you the truth, Dad seemed glad that I had lied to him.

You should have heard him talk about what it means to be a Christian."

"I know how that is, Hal. I've heard fellows talk that way. But that's something you can't change now."

He hesitated for a minute. "If you are sincerely sorry for what you've done, and if you apologized to your dad and asked his forgiveness, you have done your part. You can't force him to forgive you."

Hal leaned forward on the chair. "Will you help me, Danny?" he asked. "I–I can't handle this thing alone. I know what I ought to do, but I don't do it. The things I shouldn't do are just the things I do."

Danny tugged at the lobe of his ear thoughtfully. "I'm afraid there's nothing I can do for you, Hal,"

Danny replied. "But I know One who can help you in the same way He helped the Apostle Paul when he said about the same thing that you've said just now. God can help you to hold your temper and defeat the old nature that struggles to keep you from doing as you know you should be doing."

A little of the tension seemed to ease.

"Tell me, Hal," the young man said, "are you reading the Bible and praying regularly?"

The Seybold boy became defensive. "I try, Danny, but you don't know what a hard time Dad gives me when he finds me with a Bible. It makes him madder than just about anything else."

"We all have excuses for not doing the things we ought to do," Danny persisted. "Frankly, I'm sure that if it weren't for your dad's getting angry with you, there would be some other excuse."

Hal's lips parted, but he did not speak.

"I think finding and taking the time to read the Bible and pray is one of the most difficult things most Christians find to do. Satan fights it more than anything, for He knows how powerful prayer and the Word of God are when they become a regular part of a Christian's life."

"You just don't know what it's like around our house, Danny. You just don't know!"

"You'll have to do as I do, Hal, if you want to grow in your Christian life and be able to overcome temptation and control your temper. I have found a time that is apt to have the least interruption, and I have my personal devotions then, without fail. That's the only way I can manage."

When Danny finished talking with the young Christian, he and Kay knelt with Hal and prayed for a long while about his particular problems. Hal got to his feet when they finished, a smile lighting his face.

"You know, that makes me feel a lot better," he said. "I think maybe I can go home and be courteous and kind to Dad, regardless of how he treats me."

"That's fine," the older fellow replied, "but remember, Hal, you can't do it in your own strength. If you try that way, you're bound to fail. You've got to depend upon the Lord Jesus to keep you from failing and falling into sin."

That night at the dinner table Danny, Kay, and Jim talked about the problem Hal was having.

"I know it's rugged for him," Jim Morgan put in. "He's been telling me how his dad treats him."

Danny got up and poured himself another glass of milk. "He has much more of a problem than the way his dad treats him."

Jim looked up. "He was telling me about that, too," Danny said. "I can sympathize with him. I have to fight, and Satan is after me all the time."

"I can't help feeling terribly sorry for him," Kay observed. "Hal has a hard time ahead. It's difficult enough for a new believer to get established in the Christian life without having a home situation like his. His father must try, deliberately, to make it hard for him."

"I suppose he does," Danny said, "but that's nothing Hal can change until he has shown his dad by the change in his life that Christianity is something worthwhile."

Jim Morgan looked up. "Boy, it was hard enough for me during those first few months after I accepted Christ as my Saviour. It seemed as though I was tempted all the time."

He paused. "Of course, I had Ron to help me. And believe me, he did help plenty. I don't know what I'd have done without him."

"I was thinking about the same thing, Jim," Danny continued. "Remember how Ron used to meet with you day after day, and the two of you would study the Bible and pray together?"

"I'll say I do." Jim's smile came back as he remembered. "You'll never know how much I used to look forward to those times with Ron. We learned a lot of Bible verses, too. Those really helped."

Danny toyed with his fork. "Why don't you help Hal in the same way?" he asked.

Jim's eyes brightened. "Do you suppose I could?"

"I don't see why not," Danny said. "You know how Ron helped you. It doesn't take an experienced teacher. Read the Bible, help him memorize verses, and pray with him."

Jim was more excited about it than either Danny or Kay. "I'll see Hal the first thing tomorrow and see when we can get together," he said.

The following morning Jim left the house a little early and went to school so he could have time to talk with his friend. He waited for Hal in the hall, just inside the front door. It was almost time for the bell when Hal came hurrying along.

"Hi, Hal," Jim said.

The Seybold boy stopped.

"I've been waiting to see you," said Jim.

"What's on your mind?" Hal asked uneasily.

"I just got to thinking about how things were when I was a new Christian," Jim answered, "and when Danny suggested I might be able to help you, I thought it was a swell idea."

"What do you mean?"

"When I first accepted Christ as my Saviour, Danny's brother Ron met with me regularly for Bible study and prayer. It was the one thing that helped me more than anything else. I was wondering if you and I could do that."

Hal hesitated. "I don't know," he said defensively. "I–I'm awfully busy."

CHAPTER 8

HAL'S PROBLEMS MULTIPLY

As the day of the big victory celebration for the winning football season approached, it was the only thing the school kids could talk about. Committees from the various classes met with the representatives of the town's businesspeople after school to work out the details. Stories of what was going to take place spilled out to the student body and spread rapidly. Kids gathered in excited clusters in the corridors at noon and before classes were called in the morning to repeat the latest information and gossip.

"They're even talking of hiring a live band to play for the dance," one of the high school girls said. "Of course, we couldn't be that lucky. We'll be dancing probably to a phonograph again the way we always do."

"I don't think so," another in the crowd spoke up. "My dad said they've tried to get a band from Kenora. They're just waiting for confirmation of the date."

The girl's eyes widened. "Wouldn't that be absolutely dreamy? I've talked Mother into buying me a new dress."

Doug Ellis was going by just then. "You can have your old dance," he called scornfully. "What I'm interested in is that football picture."

In addition to a movie and a dance there were to be games, a parade, and a host of other activities. Doug Ellis, however, paid little attention to anything other than the afternoon movie. At every opportunity he got Hal off in one comer and tried to pressure him into going.

"This isn't just any old picture, Hal," he informed the young Christian. "This is really going to be something great. I talked with a guy who saw it in Winnipeg last week. He says it's one of the very best pictures he's ever seen. I tell you, you just can't miss it. You've got to go with me.

Hal swallowed hard and looked away. He did not answer his friend.

"If you stay away from this picture, you're stupid," Doug continued. "That's what you'll be, stupid. You don't know what you're missing."

Hal started to edge away, uncomfortably. "I went over and talked with Kay yesterday after school, Doug. She says that she and Danny feel it is much better for a Christian not—not to go to shows. I—I don't believe I'll go with you."

Doug Ellis grasped his arm and held him. "Do you do your own thinking?" he demanded. "Or do you let Danny and Kay do it for you?"

Hal looked away.

"You promised me that you'd go to this one show with me, remember?"

Hal's lips twitched and he fumbled for words. "That was only if you'd go to young people's with me," he countered. "We made a deal and you didn't keep your end of the bargain."

"Now wait a minute!" Doug Ellis snorted. "Wait a minute. I was over at your place all set to go with you to church that night. Your old man wouldn't let you go because you lied to him. Isn't that right?"

Color flooded Hal's cheeks.

"I don't blame you for lyin' to your old man if you can get away with it," Doug went on. "I'd have done the same thing. The bad part was that you had to get caught."

Hal's lips parted in protest, but the words died unspoken.

"It's not my fault that you couldn't go to church that night," his companion pressed. "I was ready to keep my part of that bargain. I'm going to expect you to keep yours."

Hal squirmed. "I–I'll think about it."

"You've got to do more than just think. You gave me your word." Doug's eyes lighted up as he saw Hal nod. "You won't have to bother about getting a ticket. I'll get tickets for both of us."

Icy numbness took hold of Hal, and he said little the rest of the way home.

His dad had finished work in the mine for the day and was at home when Hal got there. He was standing at the sink washing his huge, gnarled hands. His heavy jacket had missed the chair he tossed it at, and lay on the floor. His lunch bucket was on the greasy stove.

As his son came in, he glanced over his shoulder and growled ill-naturedly. "Shut that door! What do you think this is, a cow barn?"

Hal hadn't planned to speak angrily. In fact, he had turned to go into his bedroom when his dad lashed out. However, his temper flared and the words spat out almost unbidden. "I've got to come into the house, don't I?" he demanded, his tone matching that of his dad.

Big Ed Seybold turned deliberately. Water dripped from his hands to the grimy floor. "Don't give me any of that lip of yours, young man," he cursed, "or I'll whup you one! I ain't standin' for any of that back talk of yourn."

"Lay off, won't you?" Hal demanded hotly. "A guy can't even open the door around here anymore without havin' you bite his head off!"

Big Ed swore again under his breath and wiped his hands on a coarse towel. Hal took off his coat and hat and hung them on a nail in the kitchen. He started for the other room, but his dad stopped him with a shout.

"Oh, no you don't! Them dishes you didn't get done this morning is still a-settin' where you left 'em in the sink. Now get in here and get 'em done before I give you what you've got comin'."

The scowl deepened on Hal's face, and he felt the hot flush of anger on his cheeks. "I did the dishes this morning," he retorted. "How many times do I have to tell you that?"

His dad eyed him with growing suspicion. "You did all of them?" he asked.

"I've already told you a dozen times that I did all of them!" His eyes flashed. "You ought to know it! You stood right there and watched me."

"I watched you get the water ready," Big Ed admitted, "but I didn't stay around to see that you washed 'em." He paused, staring hard at his son. "You're sure you ain't got 'em stashed away somewhere?"

Hal's lips curled in bitterness. "For cryin' out loud, Dad!" he exploded. "How many times do I have to tell you that I did the dishes before I went to school. Can't you believe me?"

Big Ed lunged forward suddenly and struck him a glancing blow on the chin with the back of his powerful hand. Hal staggered and almost went down. For a moment or two he rubbed his jaw. A welt rose where his dad had struck.

He cowered in silence, but with eyes flashing hatred.

"That'll learn you not to get so high and mighty with me!" Big Ed snarled. "I ain't takin' any more lip offen you! You'd just as well find that out now."

He threw the towel on the stand beside the washbasin. "If you hadn't lied to me b'fore," he continued, "I wouldn't be doubtin' you when you tell me something. You told me you had put them storm windows on, too. Didn't have more'n half of them on. I caught you red-handed."

He laughed. "I sure found out there wasn't nothin' to that religion business you and that Orlis character have been spoutin' at me," he went on triumphantly. "It makes mighty pretty talk. Mighty pretty. But I sure found out that it don't mean a thing when you think it'll help you a little to lie."

Hal inched away, watching his dad for some sign that he might be ready to strike him again. "I–I know I did wrong when I lied to you, Dad," he said, struggling to control the anger in his voice. "I've told you how sorry I've been that I did it. And I've promised that I'd never do it again."

Big Ed leered at him. "Never do it again?" he echoed. "Now don't give me that stuff! I know better. You'll lie every chance you get if you think it'll help you get what you want. You can't kid me."

* * *

For the past two weeks Danny Orlis had not been able to fly. With the approach of winter, ice was forming on the lakes, making it impossible to use floats. It was not strong enough yet to sustain a plane with skis, so there was nothing to do but wait. He did some work on the plane's radio and spent the rest of the time studying for his aircraft and engine mechanics examination.

That evening Kay, who had been sitting across from him, her Bible open on her lap, looked up. "When are you going to take the tests, Danny?" she asked.

He put aside the thick textbook on aircraft structure. "I can take them most any time," he said, "but I'm not sure that I'm ready yet. It's tough to get an A and E license. I've got to do a lot more studying before I risk taking the tests."

He turned back to his book and Kay picked up her Bible. In a minute or two she laid it on her lap and smiled wistfully. "Now that you can't do any flying for a while," she began, "I certainly would like to get down to Angle Inlet for a while and visit the folks. The past few days I've been terrible lonesome for them. Do you realize how long it's been since we've been there?"

Danny nodded. "It's strange, but I was thinking the same thing this afternoon. We haven't been there since we started on this job, but we just can't get away right now. Jim's in school and we wouldn't be able to go home and leave him here."

"I know that," she replied. "And I wouldn't want to take him out of school to go visiting. He's doing so well now it would be a shame to risk having him get behind."

Danny sighed deeply. "If we were back in the States, we'd be going home in a few days. There'd be a Thanksgiving vacation."

"That's right. I'd almost forgotten it. We've already observed Thanksgiving."

Danny crossed to the window and for a time looked out into the darkness. Kay came and stood beside him.

"You know," he said thoughtfully, "when I was a kid at home, I used to think how great it would be to be grown up so I could do as I pleased."

He grinned. "Now that I'm grown up, I've come to see that nobody gets to do exactly as he pleases."

Kay nodded. "Especially a Christian who is living for Christ," she added.

Danny put his arm around her and drew her close to him. "It's not going to be long until Christmas. We'll see the folks then."

* * *

The night before the all-school victory celebration Hal Seybold had difficulty in thinking about anything else but his home situation. He got out his Bible and tried to read, but the words seemed to run together on the page. His head throbbed.

His dad looked over at him. "Now what're you doin'?" he demanded.

Hal did not answer. "I asked you what you're doin'!" Big Ed snapped. "I ain't goin' to ask you again."

"I'm readin' my Bible. What does it look like I'm doing?"

Ed Seybold swore savagely. "I ought to take a club to you! I ought to teach you how you ought to act! Now put that thing away and get to bed!"

Hal glared at him, venom in his look, but he got up and went into the bedroom.

CHAPTER 9

JIM BRINGS AN ACCUSATION

There was a long line of fellows and girls at the theater when Hal Seybold and Doug Ellis arrived. Those who knew Hal stared, surprise on their faces.

"What are you doing here?" one of them asked. "I thought you quit going to shows when you got religion."

Hal looked away quickly, but there was triumph in Doug's laugh.

"He didn't really quit," the Ellis boy countered. "He just quit going whenever Danny Orlis is looking – if you know what I mean."

Laughter rippled across the crowd. Hal looked down, his cheeks flaming.

At that moment the theater door opened, and the kids surged in, talking and laughing excitedly.

"Come on, Hal," Doug urged. "We've got to hurry to get a good seat."

The young Christian made no move to follow. "I–I told you I'd go, Doug," he said, "but I can't do it."

"Sure you can. You're not going to back out now. It won't hurt you to see just one little old show. You and I used to go all the time." He took hold of Hal's arm. "Don't let what I said bother you. I was just kidding."

"But I–I've testified to all the kids," Hal protested. "I've told them that I don't go to shows anymore and why. They know I shouldn't be here."

"Don't be a dope," Doug scoffed. "I can tell you one thing. They admire you a lot more now since they've seen that you do have nerve enough to have a little fun. Why, I wouldn't be surprised if half that bunch would be out to young people's next week. You don't know what an effect this is going to have."

Hal started to protest, but Doug paid no attention. He took him by the arm and led him into the theater. They were ushered to seats about halfway down. Hal took the second seat and Doug sat next to the aisle.

"Boy, I can hardly wait," the Ellis boy said. "This is going to be a great show."

As Hal sat there, he remembered that Danny and Kay Orlis didn't go to the theater, and he thought of the reasons they gave him. Jim Morgan didn't go, either, and it didn't seem to be just because Danny and Kay disapproved. Jim seemed to have convictions of his own. That was one thing that bothered Hal more than anything else. Until today Hal had thought that he had convictions about going to shows, too.

There had been a time when he enjoyed shows as much as anyone. Now there seemed to be so many things on the screen that glorified sin that his cheeks burned with shame.

The kids all laughed at the sight of a man who was so drunk he stumbled and fell down the bleachers during the game. Hal thought about his dad. That wasn't so funny when it happened at home, or when he had to hide from his drunken dad to keep from being beaten.

Hal couldn't stand to see the rest of the picture. "I've got to go, Doug," he blurted suddenly.

"Oh, no you don't. You're staying right here. The show's just getting good."

"I can't stay, Doug." He tried to keep his voice down so the others would not hear.

His companion refused to let him out. "Sit down," Doug whispered, embarrassed at the sudden confusion. "You're bothering everybody."

"I can't stay, Doug. I–I shouldn't have come in the first place."

"You're making a fool out of both of us," he repeated. "Sit down and be quiet or they'll throw both of us out."

Doug put his feet on the seat ahead so the Seybold boy could not get out. Reluctantly Hal sat down and closed his eyes.

Finally, the show was over. The lights came on, and Hal and Doug got to their feet with the others and filed outside.

"Boy, that was an awesome show," Doug said for the third or fourth time. "Now aren't you glad that you came along?"

"No, Doug," Hal told him firmly. "I should never have told you that I'd come. I don't think a Christian belongs in a place like this, and with God's help I'm not going again."

Doug Ellis snickered. "That's one I'll have to see. I'll make a little bet with you that you'll be back next Saturday afternoon just like the rest of us.

Hal left him and hurried back to the little company house where he lived with his father. The streets were full of kids, but he kept his gaze fastened on the ground so he would not have to speak to anyone.

When he got home that afternoon, his dad was just coming in from work. They met at the front door.

"Where've you been?" Big Ed demanded. "How come you ain't got dinner ready?"

Hal edged by his father and hung his coat and hat on a nail in the kitchen.

"I'm sorry, Dad, but I thought I told you where I was going," he began reluctantly. "Today was the big victory celebration for the football team. We had some–some special things instead of school."

Big Ed eyed him suspiciously. "You're lyin' to me again. You weren't at no celebration. You just used that as an excuse so you could go over to see that Orlis guy."

"No, I'm not, Dad. Honest, I'm not. I was at the celebration."

He fished something out of his pocket. "Here, this will prove it."

He handed Big Ed the ticket stub that showed he had been at the theater. His dad took it and for a moment he said nothing.

Then he snorted derisively. "I thought you told me that you didn't go to shows," he challenged. "You absolutely refused to go the time I tried to send you."

He laughed boisterously. "But then, I should have expected this. This high-sounding religion you've been spouting at me sure lets a fellow lie and do a lot of other things, doesn't it? Only he tries to hide them."

Hal felt weak and a cold wave chilled him. "I–I'm sorry I went, Dad," he said. "I'm awfully sorry. I really didn't enjoy it and – I'm never going again."

"Now you don't expect me to believe that, do you?"

"Honest, Dad. I only went because Doug said he'd go to church with me if I would go to the show."

Big Ed swaggered into the living room and dropped to a chair, still smirking.

Miserably, Hal Seybold went into the other room.

* * *

The next morning on the way to school, Doug called out to Jim Morgan. "Hi, wait a second."

"I'm a little slow this morning," Jim said pleasantly. "I thought you'd already be in school by this time."

"I would have been, but I've been waiting for you.

They started up the sidewalk together toward the big brick building.

"You sure missed a swell show yesterday afternoon," Doug said. "You should have been there."

Jim's smile was good-natured. "I don't go to shows anymore."

Doug laughed. "That's the way Hal used to talk," he said, "but you should've seen him yesterday. He sure enjoyed the show."

Jim Morgan stopped and turned to face his companion. "Hal wasn't there," he retorted loyally.

"Sure, he was there. If you don't believe it, ask him. He'll tell you. He was right there with the rest of us waiting for the front door to open so he would be sure to get a good seat."

Jim winced as though Doug had slapped him, and an ache came into his heart.

Doug looked directly at him. "You roped old Hal into being religious for a little while," he said, "but just you wait. In another month you'll never know he ever was a Christian."

That day in school Hal Seybold was all that Jim could think about. At first, he had been so sure that it couldn't be true. So sure that Doug was only taunting him. However, one look at Hal in the corridor at school that morning and Jim knew that Doug had not lied. His eyes met Hal's, and his friend seemed to shrink away and hurry to his next class.

Jim's temper flared. That was one thing that made

it so hard to win others to Christ. Christians who ought to know better were always compromising with the things of the world.

Wait until he talked with Hal. Just wait! He'd tell him a few things!

* * *

Danny Orlis wasn't flying that day, so he lingered a while after breakfast before going out to the airport to spend some time with the licensed mechanic there. Kay sat down across the table and folded her hands.

"Do you realize that next Thursday is Thanksgiving, Danny?" she asked.

He nodded. "I've been trying not to think about it," he said. "We won't be able to go back to Angle Inlet."

"I know we won't be able to go home, even though that's what we want to do," she answered, "but don't you think we ought to do something here?"

He sipped his coffee slowly. "When you get that tone in your voice, I know you've already got something worked out. Just what is it that you've planned?"

"Nothing, really," she answered. "Only I thought it would be nice to invite Hal and his father over for Thanksgiving. I think they would enjoy it."

Danny was not so sure. "Even if Big Ed would come, I don't think he could. The mine will be working all day Thursday."

"We could ask them over on Sunday then," she

persisted. "Maybe we could even get Big Ed to go to church." Kay got up and poured Danny another cup of coffee. "It certainly wouldn't hurt to invite him. He might just be lonesome enough to come."

Danny's grin widened. "I'll stop by the house on the way home from the airport this evening and see what he has to say."

* * *

At school Jim Morgan tried to talk with Hal alone, but Hal tried just as hard to stay out of his way. At noon Hal bolted out of school as soon as the bell sounded.

It was not until school was over for the day that he finally was able to catch him.

When the final bell rang Jim got his coat and hurried down to the front door where he stood waiting. Hal was one of the last ones out of the building. As he approached the door Jim stepped out and confronted him. "Hi." Jim's voice was taut and unfriendly.

"Oh, I–I didn't know you were here." The color came up into Hal's cheeks.

"I'll bet you didn't. I'll just bet you didn't," Jim snapped. "You've been ducking me all day. What's the matter, are you afraid to talk to me?"

They stepped out into the chill November air. The sun was almost down, and the sky was gray and foreboding.

For the space of a minute or two neither of them

spoke. Once or twice Hal cleared his throat and glanced over at Jim, but that was all. Finally, Jim spoke.

"I was talking to Doug Ellis this morning."

"I–I know," Hal stammered.

"What sort of a testimony do you think you're going to have?" Jim demanded self-righteously. "What are the other kids going to think when they find out you talk about one thing and live another? They'll be making fun of Danny, Kay, and me."

"I–" Hal began.

"Or don't you care what people think?"

"I've–I've felt terrible ever since I went, Jim," the other boy said. "I've prayed and prayed. I've asked God to forgive me."

"Sure," Jim Morgan countered. "After you've already done it. You should hear what the kids are saying. It's all because you think you're too busy to have prayer and read the Bible every day. That's why. The rest of us have to suffer for it!"

Jim's voice rose indignantly.

CHAPTER 10

JIM HAS A LESSON TO LEARN

Jim and Hal faced each other on the sidewalk in front of the Orlis home. Fire shone in Jim's eyes. Hal squirmed uncomfortably. "I–I've got to be going," he said at last. "I've got things to do."

Jim's gaze did not waver. "Just remember what I told you."

Hal started away just as Danny Orlis came striding up, a broad smile lighting his face. "Hi, fellows," he sang out.

Hal looked up and, flushing scarlet, murmured something, and hurried down the street.

Danny watched until he turned the comer, then glanced curiously at his companion. "What was the matter with Hal?" he asked. "Were you two having an argument?"

"Not exactly." Jim's temper still mounted. "I think he's got a guilty conscience. If he hasn't, he ought to have it."

They went into the house together and took off their coats.

"Just what do you mean by that?" Danny asked.

The Morgan boy hesitated. "I don't think you'd believe it if I told you, Danny," he said. "I didn't believe it at first, but it's true."

They sat down in the living room, and Danny Orlis leaned back and crossed his legs comfortably. "Why don't you try me and see whether or not I believe it?" he suggested.

Jim leaned forward and, without realizing it, he spoke in softer tones. "Do you know what Hal did yesterday?" He paused a moment. "He went to the show with Doug Ellis and all the other kids. He went to the show! And he's been trying to pass himself off as a good Christian!"

Kay came into the room just then. Her soft blue eyes reflected concern. "I'm so sorry to hear that," she said.

"So was I. I couldn't think of anything else all day," Jim went on. "But believe me, I let him know what I thought about it. I really told him off! I had him understand that if he's going to call himself a Christian, he's going to have to live like one. I'm not going to have him making a laughingstock out of us and our testimonies."

He took a deep breath, then continued. "I really gave it to him. When I got through, he knew he'd been talked to!"

"Oh, Jim!" Kay exclaimed. "You didn't!"

The disapproval in her voice startled him. "I sure

did," he countered defensively. "Somebody had to say something to him. We couldn't have everyone in town laughing at us and at other Christians just because he doesn't live the way a Christian ought to live. I told him he was going to have to straighten up and get his life cleaned up, or we weren't going to have anything to do with him."

Danny uncrossed his legs and straightened himself in the chair. It was a moment or two before he spoke. "Do you think that was wise, Jim?" he asked.

"I don't know why not. You ought to hear how the kids at school are talking. It's terrible."

Danny cleared his throat. 'When the Pharisees brought the sinning woman to Jesus, He condemned her sin but He didn't condemn her. He told her to go and sin no more, but he was kind and understanding. You know God loves the sinner, even though He hates his sin."

Jim bristled. "But Hal's a Christian," he countered defensively. "He knows better."

"We all know better than to sin," Danny reminded him. "Even the most primitive native in the jungle of Africa has some idea of sin and knows he ought to stay away from it. When a person sins, especially a new Christian, we ought to be very slow to criticize and condemn. We ought to pray for those who stumble and fall. We should try to encourage them to put their trust in Christ to help them live the way a Christian should."

Jim looked from Danny to Kay and back again. "But I thought you didn't approve of going to shows," he said.

"I don't," Danny told him. "I feel that as Christians we should not go to shows. But Hal needs help and encouragement from his Christian friends. We've got to help him want to live a separated life. Right now, we've got to show ourselves as friends."

Kay nodded her agreement. "It isn't that we think he did the right thing," she said. "Far from it. But if we don't stand beside him, he's in danger of getting so discouraged he might think it's impossible for him to live a dedicated Christian life. If that happens, he will keep going deeper than ever into sin."

Jim pursed his lips thoughtfully. "I–I'd never thought of it quite that way."

That night after dinner Jim went directly to his room to study. He had a stack of homework to do, but the words blurred on the pages and his mind wandered. Finally, he shoved his books aside and went to the window where he stood staring out into the night.

It had been snowing since dark, and a thin, filmy covering blanketed the lawn and the wide graveled street. Ordinarily, that would have been enough to send him scurrying into the garage for his skis, but that night he did not even think of them.

Hal was the one who had done something wrong. Not him. Why did Danny and Kay have to jump on him the way they did? A person would have thought he had been the one who had gone to the show, instead of Hal. It just wasn't fair.

If Hal didn't straighten up and start living the

way he should, every Christian in town would be a laughingstock.

Grimly Jim turned back to his desk and tried to focus his mind on his studies. It was useless. At last, he closed his books and went to bed, his homework only half completed.

Still, sleep would not come. He could still see the hurt, bewildered look on Hal's face. He could still see the shame. And, instead of trying to help him and encourage him, he had ripped into Hal savagely, making him feel worse than he had felt before.

Jim sat upright in bed and stared into the darkness.

What if God had treated him that way every time he had sinned? What if people had turned on him every time he fell short of what they thought he ought to be? He saw then for the first time what Danny and Kay had been trying to make him understand.

He got out of bed and knelt in prayer, confessing his own sin.

The following morning he was up before either Danny or Kay. A half hour before he usually went to school he got into his coat and went over to Hal's house.

Big Ed had already gone to work in the mine and Hal was standing at the kitchen sink, his young face somber and unsmiling.

"I–I'd like to talk with you for a couple of minutes, Hal," Jim said, stammering.

The other boy swallowed hard and his cheeks colored. "Go ahead. Give it to me. I've got it coming."

Jim sat down on a straight-backed chair near the kitchen door. "I did something yesterday that was terribly wrong, Hal," he said. "Will you forgive me?"

The Seybold boy stared at him. "What are you talking about, Jim? I'm the one who did wrong."

"I know, but I didn't have any right to talk with you the way I did – as though I'm so perfect and you're so wicked. God forgives each of us, regardless of what we've done, if we only come to Him and confess our sin."

He took a deep breath. "There's so much that's wrong with me," he continued, "that I certainly have no right to talk to anyone the way I talked to you."

Hal's lips trembled, and for a moment he could not trust himself to speak. "You don't know how terrible I've felt these last couple of days," he said. "It seems as though there's no use in my ever trying to live a Christian life. Regardless of how hard I try, I always do the wrong thing."

"The Bible tells us that when we sin, God is faithful to forgive us," Jim reminded him. "That is, if we ask Him."

The look in Hal's eyes brightened noticeably. He came over and sat down across from Jim. "Is that really true?" he asked.

"It's true, all right. Let's get your Bible and see exactly what God has to say about it."

Hal went into his bedroom and returned a moment later with his Bible.

"Why don't you pull your chair up to the table," he suggested, "then we can both look at it."

Jim opened the Bible to one passage of Scripture after another, reading them and explaining what they meant. Now and then, Hal asked questions. At last Jim looked down at his watch. "Say, do you know what time it is?"

"We're going to have to hurry or we'll be late for school."

He closed the Bible and left it on the kitchen table.

"I had no idea the Bible could be so interesting," Hal said when they were on their way. "And I sure didn't know it had so many wonderful things in it. If a fellow knew what is in the Bible, there wouldn't be any reason for him not to know what God wants him to do, would there?"

"That's right."

"I was sorry we had to quit," Hal said wistfully.

Jim looked his way quickly. "We can get together again to study, if you'd like," Jim suggested. "There's no reason why we have to quit."

Hal stopped suddenly. "Is this what you meant by meeting with me for Bible study?" he asked.

"That's right. Of course, we would want to have some time for memorizing verses and for praying too, but that's the way Ron and I used to do. And I can tell you, it sure helped me a lot."

His companion grinned. "That sounds like a great idea. When can we get together?"

CHAPTER 11

LATE FOR DINNER

Although both Danny and Kay Orlis were some-what doubtful that Big Ed Seybold would actually come to their house for Sunday dinner, he seemed glad because they had asked him.

"Nope," he said, in response to Danny's question about church, "I won't go to church with you. People would faint if I showed up. But if you want me and Hal to come over for dinner, I guess maybe we can make it."

"We'd like to have you come to church, but if you don't feel that you want to do that," Danny said, "come for dinner anyway."

Kay bought a large chicken from one of their country friends and fixed a typical Thanksgiving dinner.

Right after church, Jim met Hal on the steps. "You'd just as well come over to the house with me. Your dad's probably there now."

A strange look of uncertainty came to Hal's eyes. "I think I'd better go home first. You go ahead. We'll see you in a little while."

Kay finished setting the table and was ready to dish up the food, but Hal and his father had not arrived. "Do you suppose they'll actually come, Danny?" she asked.

"Sure, they will. Big Ed isn't foolish enough to turn down a dinner."

Kay noted the time. "But it's after one," she said. "Why don't you and Jim go over and see what's keeping them?"

Danny and the Morgan boy walked through the newly fallen snow to the place where Big Ed and Hal lived.

"What do you suppose is wrong?" Jim asked.

"Nothing," Danny replied. "At least I hope there's nothing wrong."

They went up on the porch and the young pilot put out his clenched fist to knock, but what he saw through the glass in the door stopped him.

He drew in his breath sharply. Big Ed Seybold was sitting at the table, a full bottle of whiskey before him!

For a brief moment Danny and Jim stared through the glass at Big Ed. "What should we do?" Jim asked in guarded tones.

For answer, Danny knocked briskly on the door. Inside, Big Ed straightened and looked about, as though stunned by the sound. Then he fumbled with the bottle in his attempt to put it away.

Danny knocked again.

Big Ed got to his feet and came striding to the door. "Take it easy," he mumbled. "I'm comin'! I'm comin'!"

He flung open the door and stared at them belligerently. "What's the big idea of bustin' in on a feller this way?" he demanded. "Nobody invited you here."

Danny ignored his angered remark and spoke to him pleasantly. "We thought perhaps you had misunderstood the time we were to eat, Ed," he said. "I told Kay that Jim and I would come over and tell you that dinner is ready."

Hal Seybold came up beside his dad. "I've been telling Dad we were supposed to be over to your place," he put in, "but he just kept sitting there and wouldn't go."

Big Ed turned to his son. "Don't you give me any of your lip," he snorted, "or I'll bop you a couple."

"Kay has everything ready, Ed," Danny said. "We'd better be getting over there, or it'll be getting cold."

The big man snorted. "I changed my mind," he blustered. "I ain't goin'." He drew himself up indignantly. "I know better than to go places where I'm not welcome. I've got my pride."

There was a brief silence.

"Kay has everything ready, Ed," the young man urged. "She's going to be terribly disappointed. Is it all right if Hal goes over to the house with Jim?"

"The whole kit and kaboodle of you can go, just as long as you leave me alone. That's all I care about." He went back to the table and sat down.

Danny turned to Jim. "You fellows go on ahead," he said quietly. "Tell Kay I'll be along as soon as I can.

When the door closed behind the boys, Big Ed made his way to the couch and dropped heavily into it. "If you're goin' to preach at me, Orlis, let's get goin' so you can get it over with. I ain't got all day."

Danny grinned. "Kay's certainly going to be disappointed if you don't come over and eat with us, Ed."

The big man snorted. "I'll bet she'll be disappointed if I don't show up. I'll just bet she will!"

"You may not believe it, Ed, but it's the truth," Danny replied. "She thought you and Hal would be lonesome, so she was the one who suggested having you over today. I certainly don't want to go back without you."

Big Ed took a cigar from his pocket and unwrapped it with great deliberation. "I've got my own way of celebrating."

Danny's gaze met his evenly and held it there. "Are you talking about the bottle you hid in the table drawer?" he asked blandly.

Big Ed started. He grasped the arm of the couch and almost stood, color leaving his cheeks. "Bottle?" he blustered. "What are you talking about? I haven't got any bottle."

"Oh, yes you have. It's in the table drawer. You put it there when we knocked at the door."

The big miner snarled. "I don't know what you're talking about. You're lying, that's what you're doing.

You're lying so you can get me into trouble. But I ain't goin' to stand for it. Nobody's going to lie about me."

"I'm not lying, Ed, and I'm not trying to get you into trouble. I want to help you stay out of trouble."

"You want to help me stay out of trouble?" he exclaimed. "Huh! That's a laugh. You try your very best to turn my kid against me, and now you're here spying for the superintendent. And you say you want to help me! That's a good one!"

Danny saw the anger flame in Big Ed's eyes. The big man crushed his cigar in an ashtray and strode hotly to the table. "I want you to take a look at this here bottle, Orlis," he said belligerently. "A real good look."

He thrust it under Danny's nose. The Orlis boy took it reluctantly.

"It looks like an ordinary liquor bottle to me."

Big Ed reached for it, but Danny moved it away from his grasping fingers. "Before you go trotting over to the superintendent to tell on me for drinking, I want you to take a good, long look at the seal on that bottle. It ain't been broken."

An exultant note came into his voice. "You can't take a drink out of the bottle until that is broken! And I want you to smell my breath so you'll believe me when I tell you I ain't had a thing to drink."

"I believe you, Ed." Danny told him. "And for your information, I don't intend to tell the superintendent anything about you unless he asks. But I know what your problem with liquor has been. And I know you wouldn't have bought that bottle unless you were tempted to drink it."

Big Ed's fists clenched convulsively. "Maybe I bought that bottle and maybe I didn't. That's no skin off your nose!"

There was a brief silence. Their eyes met on the narrow battlefield between them.

"Give me that bottle!" he cried.

Danny shook his head. "If I do," he answered, "you'll drink it, and that will be the ruin of you. All of these weeks that you've been fighting liquor will have been wasted. You'll lose your job and you and Hal will be out with nothing to live on."

Big Ed Seybold's breath whistled out in one long, thin blast. The fire in his eyes flickered and died. When he spoke, his voice was weak and faltering."

"I've tried to fight it, Orlis," he admitted at last. "You'll never know how hard I've tried, but it's no use."

"I could see that you'd been fighting, Ed, when we came up on the porch. That's why I sent the boys on home. I want to help you. Believe me."

The big miner did not move, and when he spoke his voice was scarcely discernible. "Holidays have always been the worst times of the year for me. That's when I used to celebrate with a bottle."

He paused. "When Thanksgiving passed, I thought I was over that one. And then you had to invite me over to Sunday dinner. You had to make another Thanksgiving!"

His voice rose as he spoke, as though Danny was personally responsible for the pull of liquor that tugged at him.

"I'm sorry, Ed. We didn't know."

Big Ed's lips curled bitterly. "You didn't know!" he exploded. "It wouldn't have made any difference to you if you had known! You're just like all the rest. You like to kick a fellow when he's down!"

Danny did not comment directly on his remark. "I'm going to pour this whiskey out, Ed," he said evenly. "Then I'm going to take you over to the house for dinner."

Instantly Big Ed's manner changed. "Don't do that! Please don't do that! Just give it to me and leave me alone!"

He reached for the bottle, but Orlis turned deliberately, unsealed and uncapped the bottle, and emptied it in the sink. Although Ed Seybold was almost twice as big as Danny, he made no move to stop him.

"You'd better get your coat and hat, Ed. We've got to hurry. Kay is still waiting."

* * *

On the way to the Orlis home, Hal glanced uneasily back to the house where he lived with his dad. "Jim," he said, concern in his voice, "if–if Dad starts to drink again, he'll lose his job. Then I–I don't know what we'll do."

"I know what it's like for you," the Morgan boy replied. "My dad was the same way before he became a Christian about a year ago."

Hal's eyes widened. "You mean he drank – until he lost his job and everything, and he finally became a Christian?"

Jim nodded. "It was worse than that. He even got mixed up with dope and got thrown in a jail. But it was there that he heard the Gospel and was saved."

The Seybold boy stopped and looked at his companion. "That sure makes me feel hopeful," he said. "And just to know that you know what it's like, too, helps me."

"I've been praying for your dad, Hal," Jim assured him. "We all have."

Hal's lower lip quivered. "Would–would you pray for him now?"

Together they stopped and bowed their heads and Jim prayed for his friend's father. When he finished, they started toward the Orlis home again, not talking much.

Kay came to the door to let them in. "Where's Danny and Mr. Seybold?" she asked, uneasily.

Jim and Hal glanced at one another. "Danny sent us ahead," Jim told her. "He said that he and Mr. Seybold would be here in a few minutes."

Almost before she could say more there were steps on the front porch. The door opened…. "Come in, Ed," Danny said. "Put your coat in the bedroom."

Kay held out her hand. "Good afternoon, Mr. Seybold."

Big Ed's eyes searched her face curiously. "I tried to tell that husband of yours that I shouldn't come over here and bother you," he said irritably, "but he wouldn't listen."

"I'm so glad you came."

Hal looked at Jim. A huge smile crossed Hal's face.

Big Ed sat down at the table, self-consciously, and waited while Danny asked the blessing. During the meal he spoke only when they spoke to him.

Hal turned to him. "Isn't this a good meal, Dad?" he asked. "It's sure better than eatin' beans and sardines, isn't it?"

Big Ed just grunted.

"Aren't you glad we came?" the boy asked again.

"I reckon so."

"Boy, I sure am. This is great. It's really great! We haven't had a meal like this since Mom–"

Big Ed was startled. Anger flamed in his cheeks, and his eyes grew cold. "How many times have I told you that we don't talk about her?" he demanded. "One more crack like that and I'll bash you."

The silence was electric. Danny's gaze met Kay's and held there. Big Ed saw it.

"There's no use in tryin' to hide it!" he exclaimed. "Hal's mother packed up and left us. Lock, stock, and barrel. Sneaked away with another man while I was workin' at the mine!"

The hurt in his face was deep. "She was no good, I tell you! She was no good!"

Tears came to Hal's eyes.

Kay was the first to speak. "I'm terribly sorry for you both," she said, "for all three of you."

Big Ed's voice was gruff. "Don't waste your time feelin' sorry for us. We'll get along!"

Danny reached behind him for the Bible that lay on the buffet. Big Ed watched him suspiciously. "What're you goin' to do?" he demanded.

"Kay and Jim and I always read from the Bible after dinner on Sunday."

Ed pushed back from the table and got to his feet. "You can count me out before you start that! I got nothin' to stick around for!"

CHAPTER 12

BIG ED GOES HOME

Big Ed Seybold lumbered into the bedroom, jammed his hat on his head, and struggled into his heavy coat. Danny followed him to the door.

"I wish you weren't going to leave, Ed. We'd like to have you spend the afternoon with us."

Big Ed's lip curled defiantly. "That would suit you dandy, wouldn't it? You can't kid me, Orlis. I know when I ain't wanted."

His hand on the doorknob, he paused and looked over his shoulder. "Are you comin' with me, Hal?" he asked. "Or ain't you? I haven't got all day to stand around waitin'."

Hal looked from Danny and Kay to his dad. "I'll be with you in just a minute." He got up from the table hurriedly and went into the bedroom for his coat.

"I'll be a-waitin' for you out front," Big Ed told him. "Then I won't be botherin' nobody." He stormed out into the cold and stood, his back hunched against the wind.

Hal came into the dining room again. "Danny," he mumbled miserably, "I–I don't like to go like this – right after dinner, but I think I'd better."

The young man nodded. "You're doing the right thing, Hal," he said. "We'll be seeing you."

Kay moved up beside him. "And Hal," she said quietly, "we'll be praying for both you and your dad."

Hal's lower lip trembled and his eyes filled with tears. "Thanks," he said. "Thanks a lot – for everything."

Danny and Kay watched the two walk up the street and toward the little company house where they lived.

Kay turned to her young husband. "Poor Hal. I'm so sorry for him I could cry."

"Now, Kay," Danny retorted sternly, "you know that wouldn't do any good."

Jim Morgan swallowed hard, and for the space of a minute or more he, too, had difficulty in speaking. "Boy, I know just what he's going through," he said at last. "And it's rough. It's plenty rough."

Danny's face relaxed a little as he turned back to the sofa where he sat down. "I guess we all ought to be thankful when we have Christian parents," he said. "We don't realize what it's like not to have been brought up in a Christian home until we see something like this."

Silently, Jim got the Bible and laid it on Danny's lap who opened it to one of the Psalms and began to read.

Meanwhile Ed Seybold shuffled along the sidewalk,

his heavy boots scuffling the snow. Hal followed him, a pace behind.

"I don't see why you had to go and spoil everything," Hal said irritably. "I was just beginnin' to have a good time."

"Go on back!" his father retorted. "No one's stoppin' you!"

"I wouldn't blame Danny and Kay if–if they never did ask us to come back to their house again," he continued. "We left as soon as we finished eating, and you didn't even thank her for the dinner."

Big Ed pivoted and stared at him morosely. "Why should I thank 'em?" he demanded. "They didn't ask us over because they enjoyed bein' with us. They asked us over there so they could preach."

He snorted his derision. "I s'pose you told 'em to get that Bible out and give your old man fits for the way he's livin'. I suppose I have you to thank for that!"

Hal's temper flared. "I didn't tell them anything about you, and you know it, Dad! You're just trying to find an excuse for acting the way you did, that's all." His voice grew louder. "You sure made a fool of both of us! I can say that for you!

Big Ed swore angrily. "Listen, 'Buster,' I don't need an excuse to bash you one! But you're sure a-givin' it to me. Keep that up and you'll get it right across the mouth! I'm warnin' you!"

He started on down the walk once more, talking loudly. "You talk a lot about that religion of yours," he snarled, "as though that makes you so much better'n me or anybody else. But I ain't seen that it's done you any good. You lie to me, sass me, and are just as ornery as you ever were!"

He took a deep breath. "There's one thing you'd just as well get straight. You don't need to figure that you're goin' to hook me with it. I ain't buyin' religion from you, Orlis, or anyone else! I'm goin' to keep right on runnin' my own life, and no one's a-goin' to stop me!"

Hal felt color flood his cheeks. He wiped his hand uneasily across his forehead. What was the matter with him, anyway? Why did he have to flare up every time his dad talked to him? Why couldn't he act the way a Christian should?

In the house Big Ed dropped to the chair at the table and stared woodenly into the distance. Hal picked up a magazine and tried to read, but he could not avoid looking up at his father every now and then. Big Ed's huge hands clasped and relaxed rhythmically.

"You know, Hal," he said after ten or fifteen minutes, "I was awful mad at Orlis when he first busted that bottle, but if he hadn't done it, I'd be drinkin' again, in spite of myself."

He breathed deeply. "I reckon I owe him thanks for that."

Hal started to speak, but his dad pushed back from the table and went to the door where he stood looking out in silence.

When he turned back his face was hard. "I'm through with that rotten stuff! I'm not a-goin' to drink anymore!"

A wave of relief swept over the Seybold boy. "Boy, Dad, that's wonderful," he exclaimed. "You don't know how good it makes me feel to hear you say that. It's just about the best news I've ever had!"

Ed swore again. This time for emphasis. "I've had my last drink. That's final!"

He sat down in the big chair near the window. "I'll show that Orlis fella!" he rasped. "I'll quit drinkin' and I'll do it on my own! I don't need no religion or anyone else to help me!"

Hal stared at his dad. It was great that he wasn't going to drink any more. Really great! If he just quit that, things would be a lot easier around home. And after a while, Hal reasoned, he would have a good chance to talk to his dad about becoming a Christian. But for some undefinable reason, a vague uneasiness took hold of him, an uneasiness that still bothered him, even after he had gone to bed.

* * *

Jim and Hal met regularly for Bible study and prayer, and Hal found himself looking forward eagerly to the meetings they had together.

"You know, Jim, the only thing I'm sorry about is that we didn't start these Bible studies a long time ago, back when you first started talking to me about it. A fella needs to spend time with the Bible if he's going to grow and find out how God wants him to live."

The Morgan boy nodded. "That's sure the truth," Jim said. "We've got to pray regularly if we are going to receive God's help and be able to withstand temptations."

CHAPTER 13

"TO PRAY AND NOT FAINT"

Hal was just ready to go to school the following morning and his father had just finished packing his lunch for his day at the mine. His face flushed with anger, he put on his heavy coat.

"Now Hal, you pay attention to what I'm tellin' you, or I'll bop you one!" he snapped. "I want you to come home right after school! Do you understand?"

The boy glanced up at him. For a brief instant, his temper flared, and he started to reply hotly, but he checked himself and forced a mild tone to his voice. "Sure, Dad. I'll be home right after school."

Big Ed scowled his disbelief. "You ain't lyin' to me, are you?"

He moved threateningly toward his son. "If you aren't here then, I'll skin you alive!"

Hal edged away from him, warily, keeping an eye on his hairy hand to be sure it did not snake out without warning and clip him viciously on the side of the head.

His father's voice grew louder. "And see that you get all that work done, too. I ain't a-goin' to be easy to live with if I come home and find that you have left half of it!"

He swore savagely. "That business of bein' a Christian is s'posed to make a lot of changes in a fella, according to Orlis, but from what I've seen in you, it ain't done a bit of good."

Hal's throat tightened and he looked away, but his father had not finished.

"Now remember what I told you," Big Ed snarled. "I want this house cleaned, the beds made, and the dishes done, and I'd better not get any excuses about why you didn't get finished!"

"I'll do the best I can."

"And you'd better have supper started by the time I get here! You ain't been doin' anything around the house lately. It's time that changed!"

Anger rushed to Hal's cheeks and he clenched his teeth, but he did not reply.

His father stood there staring at him. Then he pivoted and went storming outside, slamming the door.

Before Hal could get on his coat, there was a knock at the door and Doug Ellis came in.

"Hi, Hal," he said. "I saw your old man leave.

Boy, was he on the warpath! I wouldn't be in your shoes."

Hal did not comment.

"If I were you, I wouldn't stand for that," Doug said. "Who does he think he is, anyway? Treatin' you like a little kid?"

The Seybold boy picked up his books and started toward the door. He was still trembling inside.

"Boy, I'd have told him off, but good! He'd never talk to me as he does to you and get away with it."

"That wouldn't do any good," Hal replied.

They left the house together and walked up the snow-lined walk toward the school.

"It would show him that he can't shove you around and get away with it. That's one thing it'd do. That's your trouble, Hal. You take that stuff from him. If you didn't, he wouldn't treat you that way. What you ought to do is let him know that you're not going to stand for it."

Hal shivered in the cold wind and buttoned his coat tightly about his throat. Even as Doug spoke to him his temper rose. It wasn't fair to have to take that kind of stuff. It wasn't fair!

He stopped short. This was the sort of thinking that had gotten him into trouble with his dad before. It had caused him to talk back and do things to aggravate and antagonize his father.

He changed the subject quickly.

* * *

Hal wanted to see Danny and Kay as soon as school was out, but instead he went directly home as his dad had told him and started to work. He was still at it when his father came storming in.

He looked about angrily. "Ain't you got that work done yet?" he demanded.

Hal looked up. "It won't be too long now, Dad. I've been working at it just as fast as I can."

Big Ed peeled out of his coat and flung it in the corner. "Now don't give me none of your lip! I told you to have it done by the time I got home, didn't I?"

Hal's face flushed, but he did not reply.

"Didn't I?"

The boy nodded.

His dad snorted. "I'll bet you had time to go over and see if that Danny Orlis was home!"

Hal rinsed the dishes with scalding water and began to dry them. Big Ed came over and picked up the soap flakes box.

"What's the big idea of using half a box of soap when you do the dishes? Don't you know that stuff costs money?"

"I–I only used a small handful, the same as I always do."

He stared down at the dishwater, noting grudgingly that it was not too soapy. "Well," he said, "it's about the only time you've done it right."

He went over and plumped himself into a chair, heavily, and began to take off his boots. "Don't just stand there!" he roared. "Get a move on it!"

He looked up expectantly, but his son remained silent. "Get those dishes done so you can get some supper. You've got to get this living room cleaned up. It looks like a pigsty!"

Hal felt color ebb slowly from his cheeks, and his lower lip began to tremble. Determinedly he fought back the tears.

How could a fellow keep his temper when his dad yelled at him that way all the time? He began to pray silently.

* * *

That Saturday Hal went to talk to Kay and stayed longer than he intended. When he got back to the house, his dad was standing at the stove, slicing potatoes into the skillet. He glanced at Hal over his shoulder.

"What's the big idea skinnin' out of here all morning and leavin' me with all the work to do?" he asked.

Hal took off his coat and cap and hung them on a nail in the kitchen. "I really didn't mean to be gone nearly as long as I was, Dad," he explained. "When I looked at my watch it was almost noon."

Big Ed snorted derisively. "Now don't start givin' me excuses. You told me you'd be back in an hour or so when you left right after breakfast. Nobody could be that far off. Now where were you? Out with it!"

Hal turned, moistening his lips uneasily.

His father slammed the skillet on the stove and

whirled in anger. "You were over to see that Danny Orlis, weren't you?" The words lashed out.

Hal felt the color rush to his cheeks, and he looked down.

"Answer me!"

The boy hesitantly raised his head. "N-no, I wasn't over to see Danny."

Big Ed studied him intently. "I've had about all of Orlis I can stand. If he thinks he's going to tell me what to do and what not to do, he's got another guess comin'!"

He swore under his breath, and before Hal could speak, he continued. "He comes around with all that talk about bein' such a good little Christian, and sayin' that everybody ought to be just like him. He's not foolin' me a bit! I'm just as good as he is!"

Hal scarcely heard what his dad was saying. His lips trembled and he felt the perspiration rise on his forehead. What he had told his dad was true. He had not been over to see Danny, personally, and that was what Big Ed had asked about. But he had deceived him in a way, and in doing that he had actually lied.

Forcibly he raised his eyes. "I–I'm sorry, Dad," he said hesitantly. "But I–I didn't tell you all the truth. I didn't see Danny, that's true. He wasn't around this morning. But I–I was over to his house. I was talking to Kay."

Anger flushed Big Ed's face and kindled flames in his eyes. "So," he exploded, "you lied to me again! And after all the warning I've given you!"

He advanced toward the boy, his manner menacing. Hal cringed.

"I–I'm terribly sorry, Dad. I was going to let you think I wasn't over at Danny's home at all, but I–I just couldn't do that. With God's help I'm not going to lie to you anymore."

For a moment or two the man stared down at him. "It's a good thing you told me the truth, Hal," he blustered. "That's all I can say! I ain't goin' to stand for you lyin' to me, if I have to skin you for it!"

Without another word he turned back to the stove and continued to prepare the noon meal.

*   *   *

During the next few days Hal got over to the Orlis home as often as he could. It was good to sit across from Kay and have her tell him stories of the things that had happened during her years in Mexico and Guatemala. He was astonished at the transformation she described which came into the lives of those who had put their trust in the Lord Jesus.

"You make being a missionary sound as though it's the most exciting thing in all the world," he said.

She smiled again. "I hope I'm not misleading you, Hal," she said. "I wouldn't go so far as to say that. Those of us who have been on the mission field for a while don't find it particularly exciting. But I can tell you this much. It's the most rewarding, satisfying life a Christian could ever hope to have."

* * *

Jim and Hal continued to meet regularly for Bible study and prayer.

"You know, Jim," Hal said on one occasion, "I can't understand why it was that I fought so hard against getting together with you in this way. Right now, I wouldn't trade this time with you for any other hour in the week. I look forward to It.

Jim picked up his Bible and opened it. "So do I, Hal. When I first mentioned it, I was actually thinking about how it would help you. Since then, I, too, have benefited from our meetings together."

A smile lit his face. "Danny says that's the way it always is when it comes to serving God," he continued. "He calls us to His service, then when we do serve, He gives us far more than we can ever give to Him."

The Seybold boy sighed wearily. Concern was written in his manner. "If I could just get hold of myself, Jim, and live more the way God would have me to live, I might be able to make Dad listen when I talk to him about spiritual things."

He took a long breath. "I don't know why it is, but I have such a terrible time keeping my temper and not telling Dad things that aren't true. When he asks me something I think will make him mad, I start to lie before I even realize it."

Jim was silent for a time.

"Sometimes I get so discouraged," Hal went on,

"that I wonder if I'll ever be able to live the way a Christian should."

Jim closed his Bible. "I heard a message on the radio one time that's been a real help to me. The speaker said that we should put ourselves in God's care; that we should commit ourselves to Him each morning, to turn our lives and everything that we think, say or do over to Him. Then he said we should take whatever happens to us that day as God's will for our lives."

He paused thoughtfully. "Have you ever tried that, Hal?" Jim asked.

His friend's cheeks colored. "No, I haven't. But it sure sounds worthwhile."

"I'll tell you what to do, Hal," Jim said, "try it for a couple of weeks and see what happens."

Hal Seybold nodded his approval.

* * *

The following morning Hal read a portion of Scripture and knelt beside his bed, even before he dressed, and committed himself and his life to God for that day.

When he got to his feet, he did not feel much different. Yet, by this time, he had learned not to depend entirely upon his feelings when it came to spiritual matters.

* * *

For the next few days Hal's burden for his dad continued to grow rapidly. He talked to Jim about it. "You know, Jim," he said, "I used to pray and pray for Dad and wonder why it was that God didn't answer. Now I can see that the way I was living and the way I treated Dad was actually a stumbling block to him. You sure can't blame him for not wanting to come to Christ after seeing the way I acted."

He sighed deeply. "I think that it's been my fault that Dad hasn't come through for Christ," he concluded.

Jim shook his head. "I don't think I'd go so far as to say that. You don't know what your dad would have done if you had been treating him differently. But I do know that people who aren't Christians watch us and seem to be much more concerned and influenced by the way we live than they are by what we say."

Hal nodded. They had their Bible reading and prayer together. And when they finished, Hal talked with Jim again.

"I've gotten more help from committing each day to the Lord and accepting whatever comes as His will for my life than I've gotten from any other one thing that I've done since I became a Christian."

Jim nodded his agreement. "I've felt the same way," he said. "It makes each day happier and free from care."

Hal waited a while before answering. "And, what's even more important as far as I'm concerned, I know Dad's going to come to Christ. I just know it!"

THE DANNY ORLIS SERIES

The Danny Orlis series, by Bernard Palmer, delivers a blend of adventure, mystery, and suspense through various settings—from the Canadian wilderness to Guatemalan jungles. Danny Orlis, an adept outdoorsman, skilled athlete, and committed Christian, employs his quick thinking, calm bravery, and biblical solutions to confront everyday problems and hair-raising dangers. Early stories focus on Danny navigating school life, sports, and outdoor challenges, while in later books, Danny and his wife Kay provide wisdom and guidance to youngsters facing lifelike situations and challenges. Having sold over two million copies, this series has made Palmer a renowned author in Christian youth literature. Palmer is also the author of the Felicia Cartright series and various other series for Christian youth.

AVAILABLE FROM WWW.ANEKOPRESS.COM